Spitt-16 Books

Presents

The

Murder Man Diaries

By

ChoppTrigg

LLC.

The Murder Man Diaries 2025

By ChoppTrigg

Artwork by ChoppTrigg @Element of Design.

All rights reserved. No parts of this novel may be reused in any form without consent from the publisher.

First edition. All characters, events and places in this novel is a work of fiction, a product of the writers imagination. Any similarities in characters, names and places are... My bad!

Table of contents

1. The teachers dark secret . . . 4
2. September 7th A day of tragedy and transformation . . . 42
3. Butcher Babe . . . 74
4. A Shadow In the snow . . . 87
5. The Body Guard . . . 105
6. The Bait . . . 130
7. The Evaluation . . . 166
8. The Forensic Affair . . . 186
9. The Hockey Stick . . . 217
10. Murder Blades . . . 231
11. The last choice . . . 265

Enter the twisted minds of killers in ChoppTrigg's gripping collection of murder mystery short stories. Each tale digs deep into the psychology of the perpetrator, exploring the dark impulses and fractured motivations that drive them to commit the ultimate crime from chilling acts of revenge to cold-blooded calculations, these stories will leave you questioning the nature of good and evil, and the thin line that separates sanity from madness. Prepare to be captivated by the suspense, the twists and the chilling glimpse into the pit of the human psyche.

The Murder Man Diaries

The Teacher's Dark Secret

Detective Shenandoah Hines, head of the Pitts County Homicide Unit, sat across from his partner, a look of confusion painted on his face. With over two decades in the field, Hines had a nasty feeling that something unusual was really going wrong in his city.

The missing persons rate had skyrocketed by forty percent, and he couldn't shake the suspicion that these weren't mere disappearances but cold-blooded murders covered up like the bones of a dead dog.

His conscience demanded answers and he was determined to unravel the mystery behind these chilling disappearances at all cost.

Bella Shyne was the ideal teacher. Gentle, kind, and always willing to lend a listening ear, Externally, she was a vision of elegance, a Black goddess with a figure that turned heads. Her intelligence was equally captivating, having graduated from Thomas University with a degree in human anatomy and early childhood development and the intricate workings of the human body fascinated her, a dark curiosity that would later fuel her developing desires.

She was adored by her students but beneath her angelic appearance lurked sinful secrets and it all began innocently enough.

Aware that her fascination with death, something that unexpectedly grew into something darker had a contributing, being the great granddaughter of the county coroner and local funeral home owner, she found herself indulging in a harmless hobby, at least that's what she told herself.

As the time went by the obsession took hold and she had no control. The power over life and death became intoxicating and it all started at the high school she taught tenth grade human anatomy, once a place of learning and growth, transformed into her personal hunting ground.

Her students and colleagues, once innocent and trusting, became pawns in a twisted game that she had created.

Her first victim was the Principal Mr. Morrow who she adored in many ways but they way he made her feel was like she was raw meet on the market for sale.

On a regular he admired her looks and scanned her body causing her to feel nasty and continuously told her that she was going places being straight forward with displaying interest in his employee sexually, harassing her every chance he got and she succeeded in luring him into her confidence, toying with his mind with the hopes of getting what he wanted but her intentions were far from compassionate as she manipulated his emotions, exploiting his needs and desires, until he was completely had him wrapped around her finger.

The Murder Man Diaries

With perfect timing and precision the murder was meticulously planned, executed with a chilling efficiency as she invited Mr. Morrow over to her estate for the weekend promising him the thrill of his life in which he kindly excepted and after dinner and drinking an entire bottle of Dusse' concocted with and elixir that would soon cause paralysis, the extinguished gentleman never knew that he was face to face with death as he slowly faded away only to awake strapped to a gurney in a very unfamiliar room.

He could see everything around him but he couldn't move a muscle or speak as he was hidden beneath the opulent facade of her two-story estate on the outskirts of the city where her sinister secrets lay.

Inside, twenty feet below the foundation behind a discreet door concealed within the luxurious basement she created a room that resembled both a dungeon and a morgue, the chilling evidence of her crimes.

Rows of deep freezers lined the walls, each holding the frozen remains of her victims.

Their lifeless forms, once vibrant and full of life, were now mere vessels of her twisted desires.

The livid smell of death lingered on the air, a reminder of her grandfather's funeral home and after indulging in her gruesome games and one of her many ways of disposing the bodies was in a nearby incinerator.

The flames would consume the flesh, leaving behind only fragments of bone and what remained was grinded up into fine grains then scattered across the beach, their fate intertwined with the relentless waves that carried them away and that would be just the outcome for Mr. Morrow who feared for his life as Bella Shyne produced a number ten blade scalpel slicing his testicles completely off his body with one swipe slowly placing them on a metal tray for him to see.

He tried to scream for help but nothing came out.

She said, "When you get what you want, your not going to want it and your desires and need for sex are about to come to an end, your going places Mr…"

Sweat formed on the forehead of Mr. Morrow and in the blink of an eye she slit his throat striking a main artery causing him to bleed excessively leading to a quick death and after placing his body into the incinerator she watched as he burned while making arrangements to spend time Panama City beach next weekend with a few of her close friends who were also blind to the fact that they were in cahoots with a high school teacher by day and a serial killer by night and as she delved deeper into murderous rampage and with time Bella Shyne became a master of disguise.

The Murder Man Diaries

She could be the compassionate teacher, the loving friend, or the seductive temptress, all while hiding her true nature as her victims were carefully selected, individuals that were of importance, their disappearances easily questioned and her second kill of the year was a calculated act, a test of her newfound power.

The Teacher's Dark Secret

Detective Hines sat his desk doing background check on The Morrow family and could find a connection to his disappearance nor a suspect.

The victims family had no explanation as to how a man of his caliber could just disappear and now they were demanding answers. He was loved by all and played a major role in the community and this left the police, baffled by the string of unexplained disappearances and Bella

Shyne evaded their line up at first, leaving no trace of her involvement and as her body count rose, so did Bella Shyne's confidence. She was untouchable, a low key killer that moved silently through the night and with growth the darkest night would eventually dawn.

The Teacher's Dark Secret

*H*er second victim was an Italian male in his late forties by the name of Daniel Brambilla who she suspected was connected to one of the mobs. He was chosen for his disrespectful manner that he displayed for women alike of all races and in her hands was his life a blank canvas upon which she would paint her very own twisted masterpiece.

The thrill and ecstasy of the kill sent a surge of adrenaline through her veins as her victims were forever etched into her memory, their lives extinguished like candles in the wind and like Daniel Brambilla, her next door neighbor, a Ceo and multi millionaire who owned one of the many foreign car dealership and the timing was perfect as she made an example out of him when she invited him over to discuss a matter pertaining to the property line which had become a problem amongst the two. He discreetly displayed complete disrespect repeatedly and being called a bitch or anything outside of her name was a no go on her list as he'd struck out and over the course of time she learned her neighbors daily routine which would be the cause of his death. She planned her execution precisely and by midnight the Brambilla residence was surrounded by the local authorities searching for the multi millionaire who had suddenly vanished without a trace along with his dog.

Twisted by his fate Daniel Brambilla's second love was barbecue. He had a passion for the grill and outside of his hatred for the young female who resided in his neighborhood, Bella Shyne knew just that and used what he loved most to lure him in.

Over small talk Bella Shyne sabotaged her grill and while he looked for the problem, with a syringe she injected her special elixir along with honey mustard barbecue sauce inside of a Tomahawk Steak designated just for him, technically a bone-in ribeye, with a cut that boasted the entire rib bone, creating a visual spectacle perfect for this occasion and at a thousand dollars, it wasn't just a steak; it's was a statement and the heartless millionaire knew it as he dug into his steak like a wild dog after taking down it's prey.

After several bites the elixir began to take affect and Bella Shyne jumped into play leading him into her estate down to her basement in route to her secret layer.

 Bella Shyne anticipated her kill as the claw foot tube filled concrete awaited. Sluggish and disoriented, Daniel Brambilla fell head first into death and hours later he was awaked by the cries of his dog as she heartlessly placed it in the incinerator alive.

To his surprise he was stuck up to his neck in set concrete unable to move a single member of his body as his arms and legs hung freely over the tub which instantly caused him to panic as Bella Shyne applied the final touches with a machete and before she released that demon, she cut his tongue out of his mouth then whispered in his ear.

She said, "Sticks hurt and so do stones but your words, they will always come back to hurt you, now may you soul rest in hell you son of a bitch."

With all her might Bella Shyne repeatedly swung the machete hacking at her prey's head and limbs until they hit the floor followed by blood that sprayed out of the main arteries in fluctuated gushes and with out hesitation she placed the head and limbs inside of the incinerator along with the dog leaving no way to identify the remains which were to be discarded by a close friend who's father owned the local junkyard.

The Teacher's Dark Secret

Detective Hines looked deep into the lives of the victims, searching for any lead, any clue that could point him into the direction of the killer.

The disappearances weren't a coincidence and he knew there was someone lurking late in night on a rampage behind this and it was during his investigation on Daniel Brambilla's family that he stumbled upon Bella Shyne, who was his next door neighbor and she wasn't labeled a suspect not up until this point and his unwavering determination to solve this mystery is what forced him to pursue this case and with his sharp intuition and relentless pursuit of justice, along with his partner he began to unravel the mystery and with the essence of time this is where Bella Shyne's perfect façade would began to crack, revealing a sinister darkness taking many by surprise.

The Teacher's Dark Secret

Bella Shyne had descended into monstrous abyss. Her third kill was a departure from her usual calculated targets.

This time, it was a matter of impulsive retribution on an elderly woman, a retired prison guard who had the audacity to display open disrespect towards Bella in the parking lot of El Jabario's country meat market.

The woman, oblivious to Bella's escalating darkness, had unleashed the inner beast for parking in handicap spot, labeling Bella with every derogatory term imaginable. This transgression would not go unpunished.

Following the woman home, Bella parked her dark blue Infinity SUV discreetly behind the victim's vehicle and once she got out with a swift, calculated move and a syringe filled with her special paralysis concoction found its mark, plunging into the woman's neck.

The victim collapsed into Bella's arms, unconscious. Bella quickly scanned the surrounding houses relieved to find them still with in the darkness, indicating that none of the neighbors had witnessed the attack and with chilling efficiency she loaded the unconscious woman into the back of her SUV and sped away, leaving no trace of her presence. Back at her estate the chilling ritual continued.

The woman was strapped to a chair, her eyes fluttering open as searing pain erupted from her abdomen. Bella with a nonchalantly calm demeanor, had inserted a trocar, a sharp surgical instrument used for drainage of the blood and embalming directly into the victim's abdominal cavity.

The woman's body, still alive, was emptied of its fluids and blood, replaced with a horrifying concoction of formaldehyde-based chemicals.

Bella Shyne had descended into a realm of unimaginable cruelty, her actions a chilling testament to the monstrous depths she had reached and just like all of her victims she made them disappear into thin air as she disposed of the body, leaving no trace of her involvement and with the body count rising, the police grew more desperate. Desperate for answers and a suspect and it didn't stop, the pattern continued, a string of disappearances, each more horrifying than the last and now the town was gripped by fear, the once peaceful community haunted by the shadow of the unknown killer killing in disguise.

The Teacher's Dark Secret

Detective Hines tossed and turned, the weight of the unsolved disappearances a heavy burden on his mind.

He was entangled in a web of unanswered questions, each victim a chilling reminder of his failure to protect the city.

The disappearance of Ms. Williams had sent shockwaves through the community, and the grainy surveillance footage confirmed an abduction, but they still had no concrete evidence.

The angle of the footage was obscured, the perpetrator's face hidden behind a hoodie and the shadows but his partner, however, had a keen eye and after meticulously reviewing the footage in slow motion, he identified a distinct feature of the dark-colored SUV as it backed out of the driveway.

 This crucial detail allowed them to pinpoint the make and model, but the vehicle was common, leaving them with a frustratingly large pool of potential suspects. They needed a tag number, a piece of the puzzle that remained frustratingly elusive.

Weeks turned into months, and the pressure mounted. Bella Shyne, meanwhile, followed the news reports with a morbid fascination.

She would watch the detectives on the morning news, their faces lined with concern as they discussed the ongoing investigation causing a sense of satisfaction would wash over her, a perverse pleasure in knowing that her victims would never be able to speak out against her however, that sense of satisfaction soon turned to a chilling realization.

The detective, during a televised interview, described her SUV with chilling accuracy. He had identified her vehicle, the same vehicle she had used to abduct her victims. Panic surged through her. Her carefully constructed rampage was coming to an end and the authorities were closing in.

The Teacher's Dark Secret

*B*ella Shyne's grace and kindness had

began to exhibit subtle changes in her demeanor.

Her once warm smile now held a chilling edge, her eyes, usually gentle, now seemed to pierce through her students.

Her once-vibrant classroom now felt oppressive, the air thick with tension and the students noticed her peculiar fascination with documentaries about death, often discussing them in detail, her voice laced with a morbid excitement and after she unalived Mr. Morrow, she would linger after class, her gaze fixed on certain students, a predatory glint in her eyes and around the campus rumor began to circulate.

Whispers about her strange behavior, her late-night visits to the school, and her unusual interest in specific students.

Some students claimed to have seen her in the library, poring over old crime scene photos, her face illuminated by the dim light.

A young, inquisitive student and star running back named Lavell Smith noticed the change in Bella Shyne's behavior towards him as she would often single him out, offering extra help, her voice soft and seductive.

At first, he was flattered, but as time went on, he began to feel awkward in her presence.

Her attention was too intense, her gaze too knowing causing him second guess what was really on her mind then one night, Lavell saw Bella Shyne leaving the school late, her curvaceous figure, lurking in darkness causing a strange sense of dread to wash over him which caused him to follow her, his heart pounding with fear and curiosity and what he witnessed that night would forever change his life and many more.

He watched as she enter a secluded part of the school, a place rarely visited by students.

As he crept closer, he heard a muffled sound, a suppressed cry. Fear gripped him as he peered through a window. Inside, he saw Bella Shyne standing over a figure on the floor with an object in her hand with a dark sinister look on her face. Lavell knew he had to act. He alerted the authorities, but by the time they arrived, it was too late.

The evidence was overwhelming and Bella Shyne's carefully constructed rampage had crumbled, revealing the monstrous truth.

The gentle teacher was a predator, a killer, and her reign of terror had finally come to an end and at the crime scene Detective Hines used his keen mind and eye for detail, he had known Bella Shyne for years and never suspected her to be s suspect as he noticed the subtle changes in her behavior as they questioned her before hauling her off to the station.

The nervous ticks, the forced smiles. He began to see that she was more than just a kind, caring teacher and daughter of a well respected family and couldn't believe that one of his very own black queens could be so ruthless without intent. As they waited for the her grandfather, the county coroner to pronounce her victim time of death the evidence mounted, detective Hines closed in on Bella Shyne needing answers on the where about of Ms. Williams as the other detective stood around taking pictures of her SUV. The final confrontation was a tense, heart-pounding showdown, a battle between good and evil. In the end, justice prevailed, and the monster was brought to light. Relieved, detective Hines sighed, the nightmare finally over.

The Teacher's Dark Secret

By ChoppTrigg

September 7th,

A Day of Tragedy and Transformation

Retired Detective Valero Orelav was jolted awake by the news report blaring from his television. "Last night was a disaster for the Townsends," the news anchor declared, her voice grave. "This wealthy and prosperous family was found shot to death by their neighbors. The entire city is in shock. The police are baffled, with no leads in sight. But stay tuned for further updates."

Halo stared blankly at the television, his mind racing. His hands, covered in blood, instinctively he reached for the Glock 17 , a modified weapon equipped with a silencer.

The weight of the gun felt strangely comforting, a familiar companion the out of nowhere where his cellphone vibrated, startling him. He answered hesitantly, "Hello?"

An unknown voice, cold and menacing, hissed, "Your vendetta with the family is your cause. This isn't over?"

Valero's blood ran cold. He had no recollection of the murders, no memory of the events described on the news. Confusion battled with a chilling sense of dread.

Who was this caller? And why did they believe he was responsible for the killings? But Unbeknownst to himself, Valero was living a double life, a victim of dissociative identity disorder.

The meticulous detective, the guardian of the city, was merely one facet of his complex personality.

His other, a ruthless killer, operated in the shadows, driven by a dark and twisted agenda.

He was both hunter and prey, the line between his identities blurring with each passing day as he watched his colleagues try to solve his cases.

The news report, the chilling phone call, had shattered the fragile peace he had managed to maintain.

The two sides of his personality, the detective and the killer, were now colliding, threatening to unravel his carefully constructed facade. The question remained: Which side would ultimately prevail?

September 7ᵗʰ,

A Day of Tragedy and Transformation

Detective Valero's life was routine, until

the fateful day of September 7th, his wedding anniversary.

On that day, his world was shattered when he lost his beloved wife and daughter who were kidnapped as they dinned at a local restaurant and later found dead.

The saying "Time heals" was just a phrase because the pain had become unbearable, a gaping hole in his heart that threatened to consume him and in the aftermath of the tragedy, Detective Orelav found solace in his work, immersing himself in the pursuit of justice.

He became a relentless detective, haunted by the memory of his lost loved ones. However, beneath the surface, a darkness was brewing, a simmering rage that threatened to consume him along with revenge.

One night, on the anniversary of the fateful day, Detective Orelav found himself drawn to the scene of the crime, where his family had been kidnapped from.

The memories flooded back, the pain so intense that it felt like a physical blow. In a moment of uncontrollable rage, he pulled out his gun and opened fire, unleashing a torrent of bullets into the crowd. The chaos that ensued was a blur. Valero, fueled by a primal rage, continued his rampage, leaving a trail of destruction in his wake. When the smoke cleared, he stood amidst the carnage, his hands trembling, his mind reeling.

He had become a monster, a killer, the very thing he had sworn to fight against and from that day forward, Valero's life was irrevocably changed.

The Murder Man Diaries

He became a vigilante, a shadow lurking in the darkness, seeking justice in his own twisted way.

The man who had once been a beacon of hope for the city had become its greatest threat, a silent predator stalking the streets.

September 7th,

A Day of Tragedy and Transformation

Detective Halo Valero, a hardened veteran of the force, sat hunched over his desk, his in-house office a dimly lit sanctuary of crime files and unsolved mysteries.

He meticulously studied the intricate family tree of the Townsends, a name synonymous with organized crime in the region.

The Townsends were not your average criminals.

They were a dynasty built on a foundation of illicit wealth, their lineage stretching back generations.

Drug trafficking, distribution, and even the clandestine manufacturing of controlled substances were the cornerstones of their empire. They were notorious figures, their name respected throughout the criminal underworld.

In fact, they were rumored to be among the "Figure 8," a notorious list of the most influential and dangerous drug lords operating on a national and international scale and Valero had a obtained a personal vendetta against the Townsends. Years ago, during his "rattlesnake" days – the intense, early years of his career spent infiltrating and dismantling criminal networks – he had apprehended a group of Townsend operatives within his jurisdiction. The arrest had been a significant blow to their operations, and in retaliation, Valero and his family had received chilling threats.

The memory of those threats still sent a shiver down his spine, a constant reminder of the dangers he faced in his line of duty.

Now, years later, Valero was determined to bring down the entire Townsend organization one group at time. He would dismantle their empire brick by brick, piece by piece, until the last vestige of their influence was erased. The blood of his fallen comrades, the fear he had instilled in his own family, fueled his relentless pursuit of justice.

Friday morning at the precinct the air was thick with a mixture of coffee and apprehension.

Retired Agent Valero Orelav, a reflection of his former self, watched his colleagues bustle about, a stark contrast to the chilling news that had dominated the morning headlines.

He had retired years ago, hoping to escape the constant shadow of danger that had plagued his career but the past, it seemed, had a way of catching up.

The Townsend murders, the brutal execution of an entire family, had sent shockwaves through the city.

He approached Sergeant Quintero's office, his heart pounding. He said," Heard about the murders last night, any leads?"

Quintero, her face grim, regarded him with a mixture of sympathy and suspicion. She said, "The city's in shock, Valero. A whole family… children… it's a tragedy. Threats are pouring in from all over, demands for justice. Understandable, of course and the higher ups of the family is flying in today. Someone out there planned this and executed them with chilling precision."

 She paused, her gaze unwavering. She said, "A heartless act, no doubt. But as we all know, people have their reasons. And let's not forget about karma. It's a mother."

She took a sip of coffee, the silence that followed heavy with unspoken questions.

She said, "The Bureau is on it, a special team scouring every inch of surveillance footage from the estate and we do know that the assailant wore a mask, gloves... impossible to tell race at this point. Hopefully, something will turn up before more innocent blood is spilled. No one know how this family... how they... affected you but I do."

Valero nodded, his gaze fixed on the floor. He knew what she was implying. His past, his encounters with the Townsends, his own history of violence, cast a long shadow over him.

He was a ghost haunting the edges of the investigation, a constant reminder of the darkness that lurked the surface of the city.

September 7th,

A Day of Tragedy and Transformation

Forty-eight hours had passed since the

Townsend murder, and the city remained gripped by fear and uncertainty.

The authorities were floundering, their investigation yielding little more than dead ends. Suspicion hadn't even remotely touched Valero.

In his mind, a chilling sense of calm prevailed. The "angels," as he called the whispers of his inner darkness, were with him, guiding his every move and with nearly three decades on the force, Valero possessed an arsenal of skills – honed through countless hours of training, countless close calls – that extended far beyond the realm of law enforcement.

Survival tactics sharper than a razor's edge had become second nature. He was a ghost, a predator moving through the shadows, unseen, unheard.

Now, fueled by three bottles of Amaretto, the memories of how he executed the family replayed in his mind, a chillingly vivid cinematic reel.

He relived the thrill of the hunt, the cold satisfaction of each bullet finding its mark and as he drank, a chilling realization dawned upon him, this was just the beginning. Tonight, the hunt would continue.

September 7th,

A Day of Tragedy and Transformation

The top members of the Townsend family, guarded by their imposing security detail, milled about Atlanta's main airport, oblivious to the predator watching their every move.

Valero sat in his Tahoe discreetly positioned nearby, observed them with a chilling sense of anticipation. He had baited the trap, lured them into the city, and now the moment of reckoning had arrived.

The second rampage, he knew, would send a powerful message but it wouldn't bring back his wife and daughter and the weight of their loss, the crushing guilt, would forever be a heavy stone in his heart.

He waited patiently, his gaze fixed on the Townsend entourage as they departed the airport, a convoy of luxury vehicles snaking through the city traffic.

Valero followed discreetly, maintaining a safe distance, until they pulled into the opulent Marriott Hotel.

Finding a suitable vantage point a mile away, Valero set up his fifty-caliber sniper rifle, the scope trained on the hotel entrance.

He knew the Townsend family would soon be on their way to the hospital to identify the bodies of their fallen relatives and in that moment of grief and vulnerability he would strike.

An hour later his patience rewarded, he saw the first security guard emerge from the hotel followed by his target, the patriarch of the Townsend family.

The man paused, a momentary lapse in vigilance and in that instant, Valero squeezed the trigger causing the elite member of the Townsend family to crumpled to the ground. A silent testament to Valero's deadly accuracy.

Back at his apartment, Halo savored the news report, the chilling sense of satisfaction washing over him as the reporter's voice, grave and somber echoed through the room, "It's a tragedy, another devastating blow to the Townsend family. The patriarch, the great-grandfather has been assassinated, shot by a sniper. The city is on edge, authorities scrambling for answers."

Months passed, the anonymous threats ceasing, a sense of calm returning to Valero's life.

The Feds, however, had not forgotten the Townsend murders. Their investigation, meticulous and relentless, had yielded a breakthrough with a ballistic match linking the murder weapon to a specific type of ammunition, a rare and highly restricted caliber. A trail that led them to Valero's doorstep.

Awakened by a forceful pounding, Valero stumbled to the door, the previous night's Amaretto still swirling in his head.

He opened the door to find himself staring down the barrels of several high-powered assault rifles.

Federal agents, their faces grim ordered him to step back. He was under arrest, charged with multiple counts of murder and down at the precinct, his former colleagues watched in stunned silence as the interrogation commenced.

The Murder Man Diaries

The Feds, seasoned professionals employed every tactic in their arsenal, but Valero, a veteran of countless interrogations himself, held his ground.

He knew how to read people, to decipher the subtle nuances of their body language, to manipulate the flow of information and during the interrogation, the lead agent posed a final question.

He said, "Mr. Valero, tell us where is the murder weapon."

Sergeant Quintero, observing from behind the one-way glass, felt a jolt of adrenaline.

She had seen it in his eyes, the flicker of desperation, the subtle plea for help as she read his lips and knew just what to do ignoring protocol, she sprang into action.

A thirty-minute drive across the city, a race against time.

She had to reach his apartment before the Feds and upon entering his apartment, she moved like a detective.

The apartment, surprisingly appeared normal and Quintero knew just where to look. In the bedroom closet, among a collection of firearms where she spotted it —

the long, ominous carrying case that housed the murder weapon.

Relief washed over her as she secured the rifle in the trunk of her unmarked car and sped away.

She glanced in the rearview mirror, her heart pounding just in time to see the federal vehicles pulling up to Valero's apartment building. She had broken the law, violated her oath but Valero, her mentor, the man who had championed her career had once saved her life.

He had lost his family in the line of duty, a pain she understood all too well and some debts she realized could never be repaid.

Halo's arrest was short-lived. The authorities, alerted by his reckless actions didn't have enough evidence to build a case, but were closing in and three hours later inside in of interrogation room Eleven Sergeant Quintero, her face a mask of grim determination stood before him, the evidence undeniable. Yet, something in her eyes, a flicker of understanding, a shared history of the darkness that consumed them both, compelled her to make a choice.

She cleared her throat, and said, "In a few minutes you'll be a free man. The investigation... it's inconclusive. No concrete evidence linking anyone to the crime and without the fire arm the case is cold."

Valero, stunned by her unexpected intervention as the federal agents began to take the handcuffs off of him, could only manage a weak nod of gratitude.

He owed her a debt he could never repay, a debt that would forever bind them in a silent, unspoken pact.

September 7th,

A day of tragedy and transformation

By ChoppTrigg

The Butcher Babe

The Murder Man Diaries

The Butcher Babe

Colette Bannerman wasn't your average caucasian city girl. Raised amidst the sprawling fields of South Carolina, where she learned to cook and loved the outside, she carried the scent of earth and the rhythm of rural life deep within her soul and shortly after graduating high school, she traded the familiar expanse of farmland for the bustling energy of New York City, enrolling in one of the nation's most prestigious culinary programs.

Food, in the South was more than sustenance it was a cornerstone of family and tradition. Gatherings large and small revolved around the table, a fragrant symphony of flavors and shared stories and being born into a semi-blended family, she inherited the culinary prowess of both sides.

Her grandfathers seasoned butchers and farmers had instilled in her a deep respect for the source of her ingredients. She learned the art of butchering, the precise movements of the knife and reverence for the animal and every since she moved to the

Big Apple, something within Colette had shifted. The precision of the knife, once a tool of culinary artistry now held a darker allure, a primal instinct, a hunger that transcended the physical, began to consume her and the kitchen. Once a sanctuary of creativity has now become a stage for a different kind of performance. It became a killing ground of blood and steel and the line between chef and predator blurred, the once vibrant kitchen now stained with a different kind of artistry, one born of a twisted desire, a hunger that could never be satiated.

The Butcher Babe

Colette Bannerman, The Butcher Babe,

had become a creature of the night, her culinary skills transformed into a deadly art form.

Her passion for food, honed by years of watching her Southern family transform simple ingredients into culinary masterpieces, burned bright within her but her path to success was constantly obstructed by Pamela Xhylds, a fellow student who seemed to derive pleasure from tormenting Colette and Pamela, a descendant of a clandestine European culinary society who viewed Colette's Southern roots and her emphasis on traditional methods with disdain.

Her condescending remarks and dismissive attitude had finally pushed Colette to her breaking point.

The final exam, a practical demonstration of butchering techniques, was the culmination of their rigorous training.

As Colette began her presentation, her movements fluid and precise, Pamela's hateful gaze burned into her.

"Southern methods so like suck," Pamela scoffed, her voice dripping with sarcasm. "So primitive and unsophisticated."

That was the final straw. A cold fury erupted within Colette.

Pamela, with her arrogance and ignorance, would never see graduation.

She would become a cautionary tale, a forgotten memory to those who loved her.

Colette, her hands now trembling with a different kind of adrenaline, continued her demonstration, her mind racing.

The butcher knife, once a tool of artistry, now transformed into an instrument of retribution.

The air in the culinary school kitchen was silent but filled with tension as the final exams approached.

Colette Bannerman, with just a week to go, dreamt of landing a coveted position at one of New York City's finest restaurants.

Later that evening, the entire class gathered at a lively sports bar to celebrate their accomplishments.

Colette, initially hesitant, found herself drawn into the festivities. The alcohol flowed freely, loosening her inhibitions.

An idea began to take shape, a chilling plan that would ensure Pamela's silence forever.

Colette would lure Pamela to her apartment, feigning a desire to discuss their shared passion for culinary arts.

Once there, she would hold Pamela captive, filing a missing persons report to further conceal her crime.

The next few days were a blur of meticulous planning. Colette, a master of disguise, carefully crafted an alibi ensuring that any suspicion would be quickly deflected.

Then, with a chilling sense of satisfaction, she executed her plan.

Pamela unaware of the danger that awaited her, fell victim to Colette's carefully constructed ruse.

Her disappearance sent shockwaves through the culinary school and her family devastated by her sudden disappearance.

Colette meanwhile, returned to her apartment. A chilling sense of calm settling over her.

Pamela's body expertly butchered was now resting in her freezer, a final testament to Colette's twisted artistry and after being nominated for the schools final cook off Colette Bannerman, her nerves a tangled mess stood before the judges her signature dish, She-Crab Soup, shimmering on the table.

The competition was fierce, the stakes high and Colette, fueled by a dark and twisted ambition, was confident.

She had meticulously crafted the soup, incorporating a secret ingredient – Pamela Xhylds. The young woman's flesh, finely ground and subtly integrated into the crab meat, added a unique depth of flavor, a savory richness that tantalized the taste buds and as the judges sampled her creation, their faces transformed, a mixture of surprise and delight.

Colette, watching their reactions, felt a chilling satisfaction. The taste of victory, laced with the bitter tang of revenge, was sweeter than she could have ever imagined.

Later, Colette returned to the familiar embrace of her family's farm, the scent of freshly turned earth, feng shui to her soul.

In the quiet solitude of the countryside, she found a secluded spot, a hidden corner of the land, where she buried Pamela's remaining bones along with a dozen more, a macabre monument to her triumph. Her secrets were buried deep within the earth and would remain undisturbed, a chilling testament to the lengths she would go to achieve her desires.

The Butcher Babe

By ChoppTrigg

The Murder Man Diaries

A shadow in the snow

The Murder Man Diaries

A shadow in the snow

*T*he thin air cut through the swirling snowstorm, blanketing the streets of Detroit like the sheets on a king sized bed.

Inside a nondescript rental car, Michael Glass, a gun shop owner and assassin from the balmy shores of South Florida, waited patiently.

He was here on business, hired by the enigmatic Spinoza, one of Detroit's most powerful female crime bosses, to eliminate her own brother, the head of the city's Italian mob.

Spinoza arrived, her figure covered by a luxurious fur coat and the biting cold did nothing to diminish her boss like demeanor.

"He's a target and I'm a target, I know that he has a price over my head and now there's one over his. I have two million cash, upfront," she replied, sliding a folder across the seat.

Inside were photographs of her brother and his entourage partying, living the lavish life.

She said, "Tonight, we're celebrating our uncle's retirement. Perfect opportunity and you'll blend in nicely as my date so dress sharp and make this clean there will be a big crowd, and no witnesses."

Glass, what people usually called him, outwardly calm, felt a familiar thrill course through him, the cold, clinical precision of the kill.

He glanced at his phone, a string of missed messages from a life he was temporarily abandoning back in Florida. Then he focused. The mission was paramount as they drove to his hotel room.

The Murder Man Diaries

A shadow in the snow

*B*ack at his hotel room, he methodically prepared. The Beretta M9A3, his weapon of choice, was meticulously cleaned and fitted with a silencer. The air was thick with anticipation, a chilling sense of purpose replacing the initial unease.

Tonight, the snow would fall, and with it, the shadow of death.

Spinoza, her eyes gleaming with a predatory light, watched as Michael Glass prepared for the mission.

The silence in the hotel room broken by the rhythmic ticking of the clock, a grim counterpoint to the deadly game they were about to play and Glass, the assassin, was a ghost, a shadow moving through the night.

His face, usually etched with a hint of amusement, was now a mask of cold determination.

Years of practice in his craft perfecting the art of the kill had transformed him into an instrument of death, a weapon for hire and Spinoza, the crime boss, had chosen him carefully. He was efficient, discreet, and above all, utterly ruthless.

The two of them, an unlikely alliance forged in ambition and greed, were about to unleash a storm of violence upon the unsuspecting city and her family.

The snow continued to fall, blanketing the city but beneath the serene surface, a different kind of storm was brewing, a storm of death and betrayal, a storm that would leave a trail of blood in its wake.

A shadow in the snow

*T*he air inside the opulent ballroom was

thick with the scent of expensive cigars and alcohol combined with conversations.

Spinoza, resplendent in a gold and crimson gown, moved through the crowd with the grace of a panther. On her arm, Michael Glass, impeccably dressed and radiating a quiet confidence, made an imposing figure.

Spinoza, to her surprise, found herself enjoying his company.

His silence, his observant gaze, held a strange allure.

There was a raw power about him, a dangerous edge that both intimidated and intrigued her, then her gaze fell upon her brother, a muscular figure with a handsome face, already deep into his third bottle of Grey Goose.

A wave of icy resolve washed over her as the time had come.

"Allow me to introduce you," she said, her voice a silken caress. "This is Glass, a... friend of mine."

Her brother, eyes glazed over with alcohol, extended his hand. "Pleasure, Glass and welcome to the family gathering."

He clapped Glass on the back, nearly knocking him off balance.

He said, "Let's get you acquainted with the rest of the team."

He ushered Glass towards a table laden with exotic food and drinks, where a dozen or so of his associates, men and female of similar stature and demeanor, awaited.

Glass, a natural observer of human nature, quickly assessed the situation, sizing up each man with a practiced eye.

An hour later, her brother, thoroughly intoxicated, was playing doe in her hands.

"Let's get some air," she suggested, leading him out onto the balcony which was Glass's cue.

The night air was biting nothing compared to the warmth of the ballroom and as they stood overlooking the city, a sense of foreboding washed over Michael Glass. This wasn't how it was supposed to go.

Spinoza, usually so cold and calculating, seemed...different. He saw a flicker of something in her eyes, a vulnerability that didn't belong to the ruthless crime boss he'd met.

Suddenly, Spinoza's hand tightened around his arm, a silent signal as the moment had arrived and just as he reached for the weapon concealed beneath his jacket, Spinoza stepped in front him, a glint of steel flashing in her hand.

The vibration of Spinoza's cellphone shattered the tense silence. A chill ran down Michael Glass's spine. He knew that voice.

The Murder Man Diaries

"Family is the tie," the voice on the other end hissed, the words laced with a chilling menace. "A close-knit foundation and if you don't handle the business...the business will handle you."

Before Glass could react, Spinoza whipped out a small, silenced pistol. The shot whizzed through the night as her brother collapsed onto the icy pavement from a single gun shot to the head.

Without hesitation, Spinoza grabbed Glass's hand, her grip surprisingly strong.

She looked around and said, "Come on." As she urged pulling him away from the scene of the crime before anyone realized what happened.

Back at the hotel room, Spinoza paced restlessly. The adrenaline coursing through her veins was a potent cocktail of fear and exhilaration.

She had crossed a line, a line she never thought she would but survival, she realized, demanded ruthless pragmatism.

Glass, despite the unexpected turn of events, received his payment in full and it wasn't long before their eyes met, a silent acknowledgment of the shared transgression. The tension in the room was electric, the aftermath of the adrenaline leaving them both breathless.

Suddenly, Spinoza stepped closer, her eyes searching his. Their lips met, a fierce, desperate kiss that spoke volumes.

The world outside, with its dangers and betrayals, seemed to fade away.

In that moment, they were just two lost souls, finding solace in each other's arms.

The night that followed was a whirlwind of passion, a desperate attempt to forget the darkness that surrounded them.

They clung to each other, their bodies entwined, their souls seeking refuge in the fleeting warmth of their connection knowing that in the morning, the reality of their situation would return.

Spinoza, her eyes filled with a newfound determination, looked at Michael.

"We need to disappear," she said, her voice low and soft. "Leave the city, start over."

Glass, his heart pounding, nodded. He had never expected to find himself in this position, entangled with a woman as dangerous as Spinoza but as he looked at her, a strange sense of trouble crossed his mind. Perhaps, he thought, there was more to life than just the kill.

He said, "With your style of living I didn't think I'll be interested in looking over my shoulder for the rest of my life, but I will keep it in mind."

He returned to Florida and two weeks later he learned that Spinoza had been murdered in cold blood.

The memory of Spinoza's flaming gaze and the chilling words of her mysterious caller haunting him and to his surprise a similar phone call shattered the tranquility of his life.

"Family is the tie," the voice on the other end hissed, the tone eerily familiar.

"A close-knit foundation. And if you don't handle the business...the business will handle you."

Glass, now the hunted, realized with a chilling certainty that he had become entangled in a web of deceit and betrayal far more complex than he could have ever imagined. The "family" he had unknowingly served was far more extensive, far more ruthless, than he could have ever conceived. A story of karma. A tale told from the grave.

A shadow in the snow

By ChoppTrigg

The Murder Man Diaries

The Body Guard

The Murder Man Diaries

The Body Guard

*T*he humid Hawaiian air was dry with the scent of coconuts and salt water. A reality check to the ill feeling that had gripped Scott Hurst who'd been living under an assumed identity for the past five years, a ghost haunting the society and his carefully constructed scam and scheme was about to be shattered by the unexpected encounter with a federal agent who instantly recognized him.

Scott, a man once known for his daring exploits as a renowned Insurance, cocaine and heroin dealer, had faked his own death, a carefully orchestrated act to escape the clutches of the ruthless Rolland's and their crime syndicate he'd betrayed back in his hometown of Cincinnati.

They believed he was buried in a grave due the fact of the life like wax figure of himself that he watched get buried in his plot but the tables had turned, he had other plans and a man plagued by a gnawing sense of unease, found his family thrown into chaos.

A series of inexplicable events, from minor inconveniences to chilling threats had disrupted their lives, a constant reminder of the unseen who could be anywhere waiting to end his life. The Rolland family's hit man and head of security, a man of great statue named Gladstone, remained eerily calm amidst the turmoil with a evil look in his eyes, an unsettlingly placid demeanor which seemed to be orchestrating the chaos, his motives shrouded in an impenetrable veil of secrecy.

Gladstone knew more than he was letting on. He knew that the man presumed dead, who had once eluded his grasp, was still alive, a ghost hiding somewhere in the world and he intended to use this knowledge to his advantage, to sow discord within the Hurst family, to manipulate them into fulfilling his own, as-yet-unknown, agenda.

The Body Guard

The Hawaiian sun beat down on Scott Hurst as he strolled through the crowded mall.

He had been living under an fake identity for the past five years, carefully crafting a new life for himself after faking his own death he had left behind his past as a notorious con artist, a life filled with danger and excitement along with a wife and three kids.

As Scott browsed through Flame's, a clothing store, he felt a tap on his shoulder. He turned to see a man in a suit, his face stern and his eyes piercing.

"Mr. Hurst, isn't it?" the man asked, his voice low and authoritative.

Scott's heart pounded in his chest. He had been recognized.

"I don't know what you're talking about," Scott replied, trying to maintain his composure.

The man smiled, a chilling expression that sent shivers down Scott's spine.

He said, "Oh, I think you do. I've been following you for a while, Mr. Hurst. I know who you really are."

Scott knew he had to get out of there and fast. He turned and ran, weaving through the crowds, the man in the suit followed close behind.

He didn't know if he was being chased by the police or someone out to kill him, all he knew he was he had to get away.

He ran out of the mall and into the street, dodging cars and pedestrians leaving his car in the parking lot.

He could hear the man's footsteps behind him, getting closer. He had to find a way to lose him.

Scott spotted a small alleyway and darted into it, hoping to lose his pursuer in the maze of narrow streets as he ran for what seemed like hours. He stopped to take a breath, his heart pounding in his chest. He had reached a dead end.

He was trapped and just as he was about to give up, he heard a siren wailing in the distance only to looked up and see a police car approaching.

He took a deep breath and stepped out of the alleyway, raising his hands in surrender.

The police officers approached him cautiously, their guns drawn.

"Mr. Hurst, isn't it?" one of the officers asked.

Scott nodded, his heart sinking.

"We've been looking for you," the officer said. "We're not here to hurt you. We just want to talk, we received a call and theirs people out to get you, they know and it's best if you come with us."

Scott looked at the officer, his eyes filled with fear and uncertainty. He had been running from his past for so long, but now it seemed like there was no escape.

The Body Guard

The air in the unmarked car was thick with tension. Scott, his heart pounding a frantic rhythm against his ribs, felt a cold dread creeping into his bones.

He had been a fool, arrogant and careless. Now, the consequences of his actions were catching up to him.

The man in the passenger seat, his face a mask of indifference, pulled out his cell phone and made a quick call.

"I've been waiting on this day for a long time," the voice on the other end of the line hissed, a chilling tremor in her tone. "Bring him back to Cincinnati and don't let him slip from your grasp. I would like to deal with him personally."

Scott felt a wave of nausea wash over him. This was it. The end of the line. His "get-rich-quick" scheme, born out of desperation and fueled by greed, had imploded spectacularly. His first instinct was to bolt, to fight, to do anything to escape the impending doom but the roaring traffic on the highway, a blur of speeding cars, quickly extinguished that thought. He was trapped. Karma, he realized with a bitter twist of irony, had a long memory.

The ride to the airport was a silent, an agonizing ordeal. He was guarded closely, his every move monitored.

The private jet, a sleek, silver bird, awaited him on the tarmac. He boarded, his stomach churning with a mixture of fear and dread.

As the plane lifted off, a familiar voice broke the tense silence.

"Hurst," Cameron Gladstone drawled, his eyes gleaming with a cold amusement.

"You faked your own death and ran, all of this... for two million dollars?"

Scott, his gaze fixed on the rapidly shrinking horizon, felt a chilling realization dawn on him.

This wasn't just about the money. This was about something much more personal. They both held secrets that could crumble major organizations.

He had underestimated his opponent, grossly misjudged the stakes. Now, he was about to learn a harsh lesson about the price of his ambition.

The Body Guard

*T*he jet touched down on the tarmac of Cincinnati's airport, the engines groaning to a halt. Scott, his senses on high alert, felt a cold dread settle over him. He knew this wasn't a mere interrogation. This was an execution.

He had to escape.

His mind raced, frantically searching for a solution. He couldn't fight, not against these men. There had to be another way.

Then, it hit him – a desperate gamble, a Hail Mary pass in the face of certain death.

As the armed guards escorted him off the plane, Scott feigned a sudden, violent coughing fit. He doubled over, clutching his chest, gasping for air. "I... I can't... breathe!" he wheezed, his voice strained.

The guards, startled by his sudden distress, exchanged worried glances. One of them, a burly man with a face like granite, hesitated. "Maybe we should get him to a medic...?"

Scott, seizing the opportunity, lunging forward head-butting the burly guard with all his might, sending the man reeling.

In the ensuing chaos, he shoved past the other guard, knocking him aside while Gladstone stood and watched.

He sprinted towards the terminal, the roar of the jet engines fading behind him but his run was cut short as he was now surrounded by more men who quickly snatched him up. It was a dead end for Scott.

The Body Guard

The air in the penthouse was thick with the scent of marijuana and the lingering fear of death.

Scott, cornered by four of Gladstone's enforcers, felt the cold steel of gun barrels digging into his ribs.

His heart drummed against his ribs, banging like a marching band against the chilling silence.

"Looks like the tables have turned, Hurst," Gladstone replied, his voice a dark whisper laced with blazing contempt.

"Thought you were real clever, didn't you? Running and hiding like a bitch."

Scott, his eyes narrowed, feigned a tremor in his voice. "You people underestimated me, Gladstone and don't forget that you were apart of this too and as usual I always have a plan."

Gladstone chuckled, a low, menacing sound. "I don't doubt that but this time there's no escape."

The Murder Man Diaries

Scott knew he was facing certain death. But he also knew that giving up without a fight was not an option.

He had to gamble, to push his luck to the absolute limit.

With a sudden, unexpected move, Scott lunged forward, head-butting the enforcer closest to him.

The man staggered back, clutching his face in pain. In that split second, Scott snatched the gun from the fallen guard's hand and the chaos erupted.

The remaining enforcers reacted, but Scott was quicker. He fired, a single, precise shot that struck one of the men in the neck. The enforcer yelled in pain, dropping his weapon.

Scott, fueled by adrenaline, moved with a deadly grace. He sidestepped a wild swing from another enforcer, then spun and fired again.

The bullet found its mark between the enforcers eyes silencing the man instantly as he dropped to the floor.

The remaining two enforcers, faces displaying complete fear. Scott, taking advantage of their indecision, fired a warning shot that ricocheted off the marble floor.

"Get out," he growled, his voice a chilling whisper. "Get out now, or you'll join your friends."

The enforcers, their faces pale, turned and fled, disappearing down the hall. Scott, his breath coming in ragged gasps, stood alone in the opulent room, the silence broken only by the faint echo of their retreating footsteps.

He had gambled with his life, and against all odds, he had won. But the victory was bittersweet. He was a survivor, yes, but the weight of his actions, the blood on his hands, would forever haunt him and he needed to disappear again.

The Body Guard

By ChoppTrigg

The Murder Man Diaries

The Bait

Detective Kyrin Kimble stared at the grisly photos of the latest homicide victim, the stark fluorescent lights of the precinct reflecting off the glossy images. Another dead end. Another life extinguished in the city's underbelly.

 He rubbed his tired eyes, the weight of the unsolved cases pressing down on him then unexpectedly his phone rang, the shrill tone cutting through the quiet of the office.

"Kimble," he answered, his voice dry. "Detective, we have a possible lead," the voice on the other end crackled. "It's... unusual."

The call was from a small, rural police department in Southern Alabama.

A tip had come in about a body buried on Clark's bait farm. A student, the informant had claimed.

Kimble's interest piqued. A student, far from home, buried on a bait farm? It was a long shot, but in his line of work, you followed every thread, no matter and without hesitation he booked a flight that night, the humid Alabama air was hot and humid and upon arrival Clark's bait farm was exactly what it sounded like: a sprawling, pungent expanse of land dedicated to raising worms and other creatures for fishing. The air was heavy with the smell of damp earth and decay. It clung to the back of his throat.

The local sheriff, a short and stout man with a concerned look on face, met him at the edge of the property. "The informant was vague," the sheriff stated, "said the student disappeared years ago. No name, no description, just... buried here."

Kimble surveyed the vast, uneven terrain. It was like searching for a needle in a haystack the size of Texas.

"Where do we start?" he asked.

The sheriff shrugged. "Anywhere is a start."

They spent days digging, the relentless Alabama sun beating down on them. The farmhands watched with a mixture of curiosity and apprehension. Kimble felt a growing sense of dread.

What if they found nothing? What if this was a wild goose chase? Then, on the third day, a shovel struck something hard.

A collective gasp went through the group. They carefully unearthed the object. It wasn't a body. It was a small, wooden box. Inside, nestled among faded letters and a tarnished silver locket, was a student ID. The name on the card sent a chill down Kimble's spine. It was a name connected to his current homicide case in his home town, a name he'd seen just days before in the victim's files. The connection was impossible, unbelievable and now the bait farm didn't seem so far away. It was a link, a thread pulling him closer to the truth about the disappearance of Debbie Hostess.

Kimble knew then that this wasn't just about a missing student in Alabama. It was about something much bigger, something that stretched across state lines and into the heart of a world he was only beginning to understand. Debbie Hostess had fallen victim to the hands of a serial killer and he need to be caught before more bodies turned up but another question stood. How did this box get here in the first place?-

The Murder Man Diaries

The Bait

The Greyhound bus rumbled to a stop in

the small town square, the familiar scent of pine and honeysuckle filling Coy Clark's lungs. Home. He'd missed this, the slow pace and the friendly faces that surrounded him.

College life at Southern Alabama was a whirlwind, but the holidays were a chance to reconnect, recharge.

He grinned, thinking about his mother's red velvet cake and his dad's love for fishing.

He shouldered his backpack and walked the short distance to his family's modest house, the porch light glowing a warm welcome and just as he reached the steps, a black Murauder pulled up, two men in dark suits stepping out.

"Coy Clark?" one of them asked, their voices flat and devoided of holiday cheer.

Coy nodded, a flicker of confusion crossing his face. "Yes, that's me."

"Coy Clark, you need to come with us, you're under arrest for the murders of..."

The words hung in the air, a chilling list of names, all familiar to Coy. His blood ran cold. Murders? He was a student, a bookworm, not a...

"There's been a mistake," he stammered, but they weren't listening. They handcuffed him, the cold metal biting into his wrists as his parents stood in the doorway watching, their faces a mask of shock and disbelief.

The ride to the station was a blur. Coy kept repeating, "I didn't do anything," but the officers remained impassive and at the station he was led into a small, sterile room, a single bare bulb illuminating the harsh reality of his situation.

Detective Miller, Kimble's partner, a woman with tired eyes and a no-nonsense demeanor, sat across from him.

"Coy Clark," she began, her voice low, "We have evidence linking you to these murders. We have witnesses and surveillance."

Coy's mind raced. Witnesses, surveilance?

He'd been at school, studying, attending classes. He had alibis, dozens of them. Ones that he knew were a hundred percent accurate. "I was at college," he pleaded. "I can prove it."

Miller leaned forward. "We know about your... other life, Coy. The one you keep hidden from everyone."

Coy's heart pounded in his chest. Other life? What was she talking about? He was a Dean's List student, for God's sake.

The interrogation dragged on for hours. Miller presented "evidence," vague and circumstantial but Coy denied everything, his frustration growing with each passing minute.

He felt like he was trapped in a nightmarish scenario where the more he protested his innocence, the more guilty he seemed and as the sun began to rise, casting long shadows across the interrogation room, Coy knew one thing: this was no mistake.

Someone had told on him, meticulously and deliberately but who? And why?

He looked at Detective Miller, her expression unreadable.

He was a student, a son, a friend but now, he was also a suspect, accused of crimes he didn't commit, facing a double life sentence for murders he declared to nothing about. His holiday homecoming had turned into a living hell.

The Bait

*T*he interrogation room hummed with a sterile quiet, a variant to the chaos swirling inside Coy Clark's head.

He sat hunched, the weight of the accusations pressing down on him like the three hundred pounds he bench pressed only this time he didn't have the strength to push. He'd denied everything, vehemently, but the detective's words echoed in his mind: "...One body, Debbie Hostess...proof...street camera..."

Hearing the name Debbie was a punch to the gut causing him to remembered the party, the cheap beer, the way Debbie's laughter had filled the room.

He remembered... flashes and faint images, distorted and hazy like a nightmare struggling to surface. He remembered anger, a blinding if a certain type of rage but he couldn't explain what fueled it. He couldn't grasp it.

Detective Miller slid a photo across the table. It was Debbie, her face pale, her eyes wide with terror. The caption read,

Victim #16. Debbie Hostess. Below the photo, a still image from a street camera that was grainy and distorted, but undeniably him, his face contorted in a mask of hate, his hand raised...

Coy stared at the image, his mind reeling. He'd blacked out, he realized.

He'd been so drunk, so consumed by whatever had taken hold of him, that he'd lost control. He'd killed... Debbie.

The realization hit him like a barbell, bashing him with every blow.

"I... I don't remember," He replied, the words barely a whisper.

"I swear, I don't remember..."

Miller's gaze was unwavering.

She said, "We know about the others, Coy. The other students. The ones you targeted, one by one. We have the footage."

The other students. The faces swam before his eyes, distorted, accusing. He remembered snippets – a struggle, a scream, the sickening thud of a body hitting the floor. He'd done it. He'd killed them all. His classmates, his so called friends...

He'd become a monster, a predator lurking in the shadows of his own drunken stupor.

He looked at his hands, the same hands that had held textbooks, high-fived friends, the same hands that were now stained with blood and began to feel a wave of nausea, a deep, visceral revulsion at what he'd become.

"Why?" he whispered, the question directed at himself, at the wickedness that had consumed him. He had no answer but he was also a killer, a monster hidden beneath a blanket of many thought to be normal.

The truth was a bitter pill to swallow, a horrifying reality he couldn't escape. He'd gone on a killing spree, a drunken rampage fueled by something he couldn't comprehend and now, he had to face the consequences.

The Bait

Coy Clark's confession was a sickening affair, a quiet acknowledgment of the horrific acts he'd committed.

He spoke in a monotone, his eyes fixed on some unseen point in the distance, the details of the killings spilling out in a chillingly detached manner but the detectives, Kimble and Miller, weren't fooled. They'd seen enough confessions to know when something was missing.

Coy hadn't acted alone. He'd had an accomplice, someone who'd aided and abetted him, perhaps even orchestrated the whole bloody affair and that someone was close to him, someone who knew him, someone who understood the darkness that lived within him.

Their first stop was the Clark residence, a modest house that now felt tainted, the air flooded with unspoken horrors.

Mrs. Clark, her face etched with grief and disbelief, sat in the living room, surrounded by family photos that seemed to mock the current reality.

The detectives questioned her gently, carefully, trying to glean any information, any hint of what might have driven her son to such madness.

She was distraught, genuinely shocked, unable to comprehend the monster her son had become as she offered nothing, no hidden knowledge, no veiled secrets and they believed her. Her grief was real, raw but Mr. Clark was different.

He sat apart from his wife, his face a mask of stoic grief, his answers clipped and concise.

He spoke of his son with a strange detachment, as if he were discussing a stranger.

Kimble felt a prickle of unease. There was something in the man's demeanor, a subtle shift in his eyes when they mentioned the murders, a flicker of something... else.

It wasn't grief. It wasn't shock. It was something darker, something buried deep.

"Mr. Clark," Kimble said, leaning forward, "We believe your son had help and that someone was involved in these killings. Do you have any idea who that might be?"

Mr. Clark's gaze remained steady, unwavering. "My son was a good boy," he said, his voice flat. "He wouldn't hurt a soul."

"We have his confession, Mr. Clark," Miller interjected. "He admitted to the murders."

Mr. Clark remained silent, his jaw tight. He wasn't surprised and he wasn't denying it. He was... taken by surprise.

Kimble exchanged a look with Miller. They knew they weren't getting anything from him, not willingly and they also knew, with a certainty that settled deep in their bones, that Mr. Clark was hiding something. Something more than just the grief of a father losing his son. Something darker, something more sinister. They left the house, the weight of their suspicions heavy in the air. They had their killer, but they didn't have the whole story and with vowed that they wouldn't rest until they uncovered the truth, no matter how deeply buried it was.

The Bait

Detective Kimble and Miller wouldn't have cracked the Debbie Hostess case without their initial lead, but the investigation was far from over. The quiet confession from Coy Clark had opened a Pandora's Box, revealing a darkness that stretched far beyond the confines of his troubled mind. The detectives, haunted by the feeling that they were only scratching the surface, secured a warrant to excavate the entire

Clark property and the judge, sensing the gravity of the situation, didn't hesitate.

The excavation was a grim affair. The idyllic bait farm, with its pungent smell and deceptively peaceful appearance, became a scene of macabre discovery. Three days into the dig, the earth yielded its secrets.

Not one, not two, but over thirty bodies were unearthed, skeletal remains that spoke of a long and brutal history and majority of them were of Italian descent they later learned.

The revelation sent shockwaves through the small town. The quiet, unassuming Clark family, pillars of the community, were now at the center of a horrific scandal and the most disturbing part was that these victims weren't connected to Coy Clark's killing spree. This was something else, something older, something far more sinister.

The detectives returned to the interrogation room, the air clustered with tension as they confronted Mr. Clark with their findings. He remained stoic for a long moment, his eyes betraying nothing.

Then, a flicker of something – resignation? relief? – crossed his face.

"I had a contract," he finally said, his voice barely a whisper. "With an Italian mob."

He demanded to speak with his lawyer, refusing to say another word.

The pieces of the puzzle began to click into place. The Clark bait farm wasn't just a place of business; it was a burial ground, a silent testament to the things money could buy.

The ensuing months were a whirlwind of court dates, investigations, and media frenzy and while the case grew, expanding beyond the small town, reaching the ears of law enforcement agencies across the country. The motive became clear: the Italian mob, seeking a discreet and untraceable location to dispose of their victims, had struck a deal with the Clarks. The bait farm, with its remote location and unassuming facade, was the perfect cover and the outcome was extreme. The Clark family name became synonymous with horror, their legacy forever tainted by the blood spilled on their land. The small town was irrevocably changed, its innocence shattered.

The case of the Italian burial ground became a chilling reminder of the darkness that dwelled beneath the surface of even the most ordinary lives and in the end, the twist was this: Coy Clark's killing spree, as horrific as it was, had inadvertently exposed a far greater evil, as he set he bit bait and couldn't get off the hook, a secret that had been buried for years, waiting to be unearthed.

The Bait

By ChoppTrigg

The Murder Man Diaries

The Evaluation

Dr. Florida Givens, a renowned and we'll know psychiatrist, exuded a perplex professionalism.

Her office, a sanctuary of soft lighting and soothing colors, was a haven for the city's elite, particularly the wealthy and troubled men who sought her help, confiding their deepest anxieties, vulnerabilities and their secrets where Florida listened patiently, her empathetic gaze offering comfort but behind the mask of the compassionate healer was a motive infused with a vengeance. Florida wasn't just treating her patients; she was meticulously studying them, identifying their weaknesses, their vulnerabilities and then, she was eliminating them and disposing their bodies in various ways leaving a trail for authorities but she was meticulous with her movement.

One by one, wealthy men were vanishing without a trace, their disappearances were chalked up to bad luck, poor decisions, or simply vanishing acts and not a single soul suspected their trusted psychiatrist, the woman who held their confidences, was the architect of their death.

Her methods were subtle, insidious. She used her knowledge of their psychological frailties, manipulating them, driving them to despair, and ultimately to their deaths.

Some were driven to suicide, others met with "accidents" that seemed tragically plausible.

Florida was meticulous, leaving no trace, no suspicion. Her body count rose, each victim a testament to her outlandish ruthlessness and Detective Stroganoff, a homicide investigator with the Thongsville Police Department, was growing increasingly frustrated. The disappearances were too frequent and similar.

He felt a nagging suspicion that something more sinister was really at play.

The victims were all wealthy, all men, and all had one thing in common: they were patients of Dr. Florida Givens.

Stroganoff began to dig deeper. He reviewed the files of the missing men, searching for a connection, a clue that would explain their sudden vanishing acts. He interviewed family members, friends, business associates but everyone spoke highly of Dr. Givens, praising her professionalism and her dedication to her patients. She was above suspicion, a pillar of the community.

Then, Stroganoff found a lead, a small, almost insignificant detail that had been overlooked.

One of the missing men had mentioned a rare and obscure medication that Dr. Givens had prescribed him.

Stroganoff researched the drug and discovered its potentially lethal side effects if not administered correctly.

It was a long shot, but it was enough to open a portal, a gateway into the dark world of Dr. Florida Givens and after obtaining a warrant to search her office, meticulously combing through her files, her records ,and her computer hidden amongst the legitimate patient files, he found them: detailed accounts of each victim's vulnerabilities, their weaknesses, their fears and alongside each account, a plan, a strategy for their elimination.

Florida Givens, the trusted psychiatrist, was a serial killer, hiding in plain sight, preying on the vulnerable, and leaving a trail of broken lives in her wake.

Stroganoff knew he had his killer, but he also knew that the case was far from over. The portal he had opened revealed not just one killer, but a network of darkness, a web of deceit and manipulation that reached far beyond the walls of Dr. Givens' pristine office.

The Evaluation

*D*etective Stroganoff didn't hesitate. He had enough and the evidence was irrefutable, a chilling tapestry woven from meticulous notes, manipulated prescriptions, and damning circumstantial connections.

He and his partner arrived at Dr. Givens' opulent office, the same office that had given off a feeling of healing and trust for so long. Florida Givens maintained her composed and didn't resist. She knew the game was over and the station, the interrogation room hummed with a tense quiet.

Stroganoff sat across from Givens, her calm demeanor a reflecting mirror to the horror of her actions and as he laid out the evidence, piece by damning piece Givens listened, her expression unchanging and when he finished she didn't deny anything.

Her voice wall dull and void, as if she didn't have a care in the world. She simply replied, "They were weak and vulnerable. They needed... guidance and a get away."

"Guidance and a get away. We have long list of dead men who left behind families and guidance in your eyes is murder in the first degree."

Stroganoff raised an eyebrow waiting on her response. Givens shrugged her shoulders and said, "They were lost. I simply... expedited the process."

The coldness in her voice sent a shiver down Stroganoff's spine. He said, "You manipulated them and preyed on their weaknesses."

Givens fought back she said, "They paid me for my services, they sought my help and I provided just that."

Stroganoff leaned forward and said, "Well for the record your help involved murder and these families will want justice"

Givens was silent for a moment, then a small, almost imperceptible smile played on her lips. She said, "They were all so... predictable, especially the ones with the sexual dysfunctions... so easily swayed."

Stroganoff's stomach churned. He knew what she was implying. "You used them," he said, his voice tight.

"I gave them what they wanted and that was pleasure. Comfort. Validation," Givens replied.

"And what about the ones with marital problems?" Stroganoff asked, his voice laced with disgust.

"I offered solutions," Givens said. "Advice. Strategies and they were grateful."

Stroganoff stared at her, his mind struggling to comprehend the depth of her depravity.

"You charged them for this?" he asked. "For manipulating them into their graves?"

Givens nodded. "

She smiled and said, "My rates were quite reasonable, considering the... results."

Stroganoff felt a wave of nausea wash over him. This wasn't just about power. It was about greed. It was about exploiting the vulnerable for personal gain.

Givens had turned therapy into a twisted game, a panel selection where she played judge, jury, and executioner, all while lining her pockets with the blood money of her victims.

He looked at her, the woman who had masqueraded as a healer, who they thought was a doctor, but really a monster, a predator who had preyed on the weakest and most vulnerable members of society and work substantial evidence he knew that justice, however belated, would finally be served.

The Evaluation

Nearly three years had passed. Three years of legal maneuvering, procedural delays, and behind-the-scenes battles. The families of Florida Given's victims sat in the courtroom, their faces a statue with grief and a burning desire for justice.

Today was the day of reckoning and Florida Givens, impeccably dressed and composed, sat at the defendant's table, her gaze unwavering.

The prosecution's case was airtight, a mountain of evidence meticulously assembled over the years but Given's lawyer was a formidable opponent, a master of deflection and reasonable doubt. He painted Givens as a misunderstood healer, a victim of her own compassion, her methods perhaps unconventional, but her intentions always pure and he argued that her actions, while perhaps misguided, were not criminal, but rather the result of a brilliant mind pushed to its limits.

For three grueling days, the lawyers interrogated Givens, dissecting her methods, her motives and her very being. Givens, the psychiatrist answered every question with a carefully crafted response, a clinical explanation for her actions.

She spoke of transference of therapeutic boundaries and the complexities of the human psyche but she never admitted guilt, never showed remorse as she continued to presented herself as a doctor who had only crossed a line, perhaps, but not on criminal scale and after the jury deliberated for three agonizing days the tension in the courtroom was palpable, the silence broken only by the rustling of papers and the occasional cough. Finally, they returned. Their verdict was inconclusive. They couldn't agree. The word "insanity" hung in the air, a legal loophole that threatened to derail the entire case and the judge, weary of the protracted proceedings, delivered his verdict.

Florida Givens would not be convicted of murder.

The families of the victims gasped, their hopes dashed but the judge wasn't finished. He revoked Given's medical license, effectively ending her career as a psychiatrist and citing the jury's inconclusive verdict and the evidence presented, he ordered her to be placed in a high-security mental health facility for an indefinite period along with a fine that was to be paid as restitution to the families.

It wasn't the justice the families had sought. It wasn't the punishment they believed she deserved. Florida Givens, though not convicted of murder, would never practice medicine again.

She would spend her days in the sterile confines of a mental institution, a place where her manipulations and her twisted understanding of the human mind would be rendered powerless. It was a twisted ending, a legal compromise that left a bitter taste in everyone's mouth.

The Evaluation

By ChoppTrigg

The Forensic Affair

*I*rish Malaccan, forensic odontologist, glanced at her Rolex as she waited at the red light. It was 5:00 a.m. and the fourth crime scene this week.

A smirk tightened her cute features as this was another opportunity being that she wasn't always on call but this week had been a relentless marathon of death.

Today's victim: another body discovered in a dumpster, the telltale bite marks piercing

The Murder Man Diaries

the crushed wind pipe. The signature of a predator that was on the kill.

The pre-dawn chill bit through her jacket as she approached the scene noticing the flashing lights of the police cruisers painting the dark alleyway in a strobe-like dance of red and blues.

 She was close friends with Captain Dae'ontre Newsome, a relationship that had escalated into more than just a friendship.

The affair had ended in peaceful way but it left an unspoken tension between the two.

A delicate balance between professional respect and personal history.

Dae'ontre's protectiveness, while appreciated, sometimes felt like a leash, limiting her involvement in cases, prioritizing her safety above all else.

As she examined the body, the familiar wave of professional detachment washed over her. She focused on the bite marks, meticulously documenting the patterns, the pressure and the unique characteristics that could identify the killer, she also second guessed why all of the victims were handsome black males with athletic frames.

This was her world, a world of teeth, bone and secrets whispered in the silent language of the dead and later that day, back in her pristine lab Irish was reviewing her findings when her phone rang. It was an unfamiliar number but that was common in her line of work.

"Dr. Malaccan?" a soft toned voice asked.

"Speaking," Irish replied, a touch of unease running down her spine.

"I know about your... special skills," the voice hissed. "And I know about your connection to Captain Newsome."

Irish's was at a loss for words. "Who is this?" she demanded.

The voice giggled, an eerily, excited sound. "Let's just say I'm ... interested in your work and may have a proposition for you."

The proposition was simple yet terrifying. The person wanted her to alter the evidence to protect someone and if she refused the voice made it clear that her past indiscretions, her affair with the Captain, her professional reputation, her very life, would be casket fitted.

The call ended, leaving Irish in a cold sweat. She was trapped between her loyalty to the law, her friendship with Dae'ontre, and the very real threat to her life.

She was caught in a maze of events she couldn't control. The neatly ordered world of her lab, the clinical detachment she cultivated gave her since of unease. She was no longer just an odontologist, she was a target, a pawn in a game far more dangerous than she could have ever imagined and she knew, with a chilling certainty, that her life was about to take a terrifying turn.

The Forensic Affair

*T*rellis Roundtree's mental battles waged a

silent war within her, weakening her spirit yet paradoxically, her physical form remained a testament to dedication.

Her commitment to the local gym was unwavering. Every morning, around 2 a.m., she'd slip into the deserted space, a solitary figure amidst the iron and treadmills and she wasn't the only one who sought solace in the quiet hours.

Others who had that same passion, those escaping their own demons, shared the gym's pre-dawn solitude and her latest victim was a striking, muscular black man. He was handsome and confident, the kind of man who turned heads.

He'd approached Trellis flirting and complimenting her figure and her strength. Trellis, despite her inner turmoil, played the game, feigning indifference but secretly thrilled by his attention. She allowed herself to be charmed, to be seduced by the fleeting promise of connection and it was her deadly game.

The Murder Man Diaries

The seduction was part of her ritual. She lured her victims in, gaining their trust and their affection then in the intimate moments that followed, the darkness within her would surface. She'd embrace them and kiss them, her touch a prelude to horror.

She'd suck on their necks with a passion masked with violence to come and with a sudden and brutal shift, she'd bite down, like a pit bull clamping its jaws shut, crushing their windpipe, extinguishing their life. The contrast of all chilling, the allure of her beauty, the promise of intimacy, followed by the savage, merciless act of killing. It was a dance of attraction and destruction, a bench press in the shadows of the early morning.

The Forensic Affair

*I*rish shook off the lingering unease from the mysterious phone call, the threat hanging heavy in the air. Her first instinct was to confide in Captain Newsome, to bring him into the loop, but a nagging doubt held her back. She needed more, concrete evidence, something beyond a gut feeling and as her attention snapped back to the crime scene photos, the gruesome images of the victims the bite marks, all clustered around the windpipe, the angle consistent and precise. It was a detail that nagged at her, a whisper in the back of her mind then it clicked.

The angle, the pressure and the specific placement of the marks… it pointed to a female assailant and the realization was chilling.

She relayed her findings to Newsome, carefully explaining her reasoning. He listened intently, his expression growing serious and he knew Irish's expertise, her meticulous attention to detail and if she suspected a female killer, he trusted her instincts. He also knew that this revelation would change the entire direction of the investigation. Things were about to get very interesting and dangerous.

Irish had access to dental records through her work as a forensic odontologist. She knew that the key to identifying the killer lay hidden within those files and she was determined to find the connection and unmask the predator, even if it meant putting her own life on the line. The thought sent a shiver down her spine, but her resolve was firm.

Monday morning arrived, and at the dental office, Irish began her search. She meticulously went through the files of female patients, comparing dental records to the unique bite patterns from the crime scenes.

Hours passed, each file a dead end, each hope dwindling. Frustration gnawed at her. She was so close, she could feel it then a new appointment popped up on the schedule: Trellis Roundtree.

The name was unfamiliar, but as Irish pulled up the file, a jolt of recognition shot through her.

The dental chart, the specific alignment of the teeth... it was a match. A perfect match. The blood ran cold in her veins.

Trellis Roundtree, the name of the suspected killer was no longer a mystery. But now, Irish faced an even greater challenge: how to expose her, how to bring her to justice, without becoming another victim herself. The game had just become intensely personal.

Irish Malaccan's discovery sent a jolt of urgency through the precinct. She presented her findings to Captain Newsome, the dental records n undeniable indictment against Trellis Roundtree. Newsome, a detective with a sharp mind, immediately launched a parallel investigation.

He delved into the backgrounds of the victims, meticulously piecing together their lives, their routines, their connections until a pattern emerged, chilling in its simplicity.

All the men, the victims of the brutal neck bites shared a common thread. A membership at the same local gym.

The gym was the perfect hunting ground where Trellis could observe her prey, assess their strength and their vulnerabilities.

Newsome couldn't stop his mind from racing. He secured access to the gym's surveillance footage with the hopes of finding concrete evidence, a visual link between Trellis and the men she had targeted.

He spent hours reviewing the tapes, fast-forwarding, rewinding, searching for a glimpse of Trellis, a connection between her and the victims and he continued to watched the grainy footage, a disturbing picture began to emerge. Trellis, her beauty striking even in the low-resolution images, was a regular at the gym, her movements fluid and athletic.

He watched as she interacted with the victims, engaging them in casual conversation. Her charm evident. The footage showed her leaving the gym with them, sometimes separately, sometimes together. It was damning evidence, a visual confirmation of Irish's suspicions but an ounce of doubt lingered in Newsome's mind.

Trellis, while athletic and toned, was not a large woman. The men she had killed were physically imposing and powerful and he couldn't see the slender woman on the screen having the brutal force required to subdue men who could have overpowered a grizzly bear. He voiced his concerns to Irish. Shaking his head, he said "She's not big enough, how could she...I just don't see it."

Irish offered a possible explanation. She said, "It's not about size," It's all about the technique. She could be using leverage or exploiting pressure points and the bite itself... it's not just about strength. It's about precision, knowing where to apply the pressure to cause deathly damage."

Newsome considered her words. It made sense. Trellis's athleticism, combined with her knowledge of human anatomy, could make her a lethal predator, regardless of her size. The doubt in his mind didn't completely disappear, but the evidence was overwhelming. He had his suspect and he knew, with a chilling certainty, that Trellis Roundtree was far more dangerous than he had initially imagined.

The Forensic Affair

*T*rellis Roundtree was aware of Irish Malaccan's connection to Captain Newsome. She knew about their past and the brief affair and she knew that Irish was working with Newsome, piecing together the puzzle of her gruesome crimes.

The phone call she'd made to Irish wasn't a one-off, it was the opening gambit in a much larger game.

Around 2 a.m., Trellis sat in her Lamborghini Urus, the sleek lines of the luxury SUV shinned from street lights but complete darkness consumed her thoughts as she was contemplating on her next move, her next victim, but a chilling sensation prickled her skin as she felt watched, observed and she was.

Unseen eyes followed her every move, their presence a silent threat.

Trellis pulled out her phone and dialed Irish Malaccan's number. Irish answered on the second ring, her voice wary.

"I know you know who I am," Trellis said, her voice soft, almost seductive. "I purposely made that appointment, just to get close to you, to see you. I could have killed you then and there, but I chose not to. Because I have a proposition for you."

She paused, letting the weight of her words sink in. She simply said, "Scramble the evidence, Irish. Manipulate your findings and I'll deposit one million dollars into your account. Right now. No questions asked."

Trellis's tone shifted, the softness replaced by a chilling growl. She said, "If you refuse... then cancel Thanksgiving,

Christmas, and New Year's because if I go down, you're going down with me. That's my promise and tell Captain Newsome... don't bother trying to find me. He won't."

The line went dead, leaving Irish in a state of shock. Trellis's words were a direct threat, a chilling reminder of her power and her ruthlessness. She knew too much, not just about the murders, but about Irish's past, her vulnerabilities. The stakes had been raised and it wasn't just about catching a killer anymore. It was a personal battle, a fight for survival and Trellis

Roundtree had just made it very clear: she was playing to win.

The Forensic Affair

The vibration of her phone jolted Irish awake. An email notification: a recent deposit of One million dollars.

The seven digit number stared back at her from the screen, solidifying the nightmare. It wasn't a dream. Trellis's offer or rather her threat, was real. Irish sat up, her head reeling. A million dollars. A life-changing amount but at what cost?

Her mind wrestled with the dilemma. Manipulating the evidence meant accepting the blood money, becoming complicit in Trellis's crimes and refusing meant risking everything, facing the wrath of a woman who clearly wouldn't hesitate to eliminate any threat then she thought about the faces of the victims' families which flashed before her eyes, their grief, a burden on her conscience but the choice was clear. This time, she wouldn't follow her first instinct, the one that screamed self-preservation.

At 10 a.m., Irish contacted Captain Newsome. She said, "I've re-examined the evidence and I don't think Trellis is the killer, her voice steady despite the turmoil within.

Newsome was stunned. "What? But the dental records…"

"They're similar, yes," Irish interrupted. "But there's a crucial difference. Trellis's left K-9 is dull, almost like a number two pencil. The bite marks on the victims are sharp, piercing. I'm faxing you the proof now."

Newsome was speechless. He'd trusted the dental evidence, it had seemed irrefutable. Now, Irish was telling him it was wrong. He admitted. He said, "I... I second-guessed her as a suspect but the dental records... they don't lie."

"They can be misinterpreted and now the chase is still on," Irish countered.

The following morning, Trellis Roundtree settled into her new hideout in Cancun, a luxurious condo overlooking the turquoise waters and as she watched the local news, a smug satisfaction spread across her face as the reporter described the ongoing investigation.

"...Authorities are still on the hunt for the person who's responsible for killing five me in five days and as of now theirs not one leads nor a suspects and as of now the case is cold..."

Trellis smiled and changed the channel, a chillingly beautiful predator basking in her freedom.

"Good girl, Irish Malaccan," she murmured, sipping her mocha latte. Weeks turned into months, then years, no more bodies surfaced in Miami. The case of the neck-biting killer went cold, a chilling reminder of a predator who had vanished without a trace but in Cancun, things were different.

Trellis Roundtree, like a praying mantis, was on the prowl once more. The killing spree had simply relocated and the game had changed, but her rampage continued.

<u>The Forensic Affair</u>

<u>ChoppTrigg</u>

The Murder Man Diaries

The Hockey Stick

Frank Myers had always dreamed of playing hockey. Growing up in the small town of St. Drake, Ontario, he spent countless hours on the frozen lakes, perfecting his shot, imagining himself on the ice gaining the attention of the crowds with his skills. He was a star player in high school, earning a scholarship to a prestigious college where he aimed to build a career in the sport he loved but everything changed during his senior year.

From the beginning his mother thought a black hockey player was absurd but she didn't stop him, she influenced him to the fullest.

It was the winter of 2025, a season filled with promise, when an unfortunate accident shattered not only his leg—breaking it in three places—but also his dreams.

The injury sidelined him for the remainder of the season, leaving him in a limbo of pain and frustration.

As he underwent surgery and rehabilitation, the world he once knew drifted away with his dreams of a hockey career in fragments, Frank struggled to find a new purpose.

He watched as his teammates moved on, while he grew increasingly isolated. The bitterness turned inward, festering into something darker. Unable to cope with the pain of his shattered dreams, he withdrew from his friends and family, spiraling into depression and as the months passed, a sense of emptiness consumed him. Frank found himself wandering into troubling places and associating with unsavory characters. The darkness that had seeped into his life began to take shape, transforming him into something he had never imagined he could become and it began with small acts of rebellion and aggression.

Frustrated with his situation, Frank sought validation through risky behavior and violence. His life took a turn when he crossed paths with a group that preyed on vulnerable individuals The alley reeked of stale beer and desperation. Frank, his jaw tight, watched as the group of men harassed a young woman, their laughter echoing off the grimy brick walls. He'd had enough. He'd seen this kind of thing too many times, the casual cruelty, the unchecked aggression. Something snapped inside him. He wasn't going to stand by and watch this time.

He stepped into the alley, his presence immediately shifting the atmosphere. The laughter died down, replaced by a low growl. The men turned towards him, their eyes narrowed, their bodies tensing. Frank knew he was outnumbered, outmatched, but the rage burning within him deflected any fear.

He wasn't thinking, he was reacting and driven by an instinct he couldn't control.

The scuffle erupted quickly, a chaotic flurry of fists, knees and elbows. Frank, fueled by adrenaline and fury, fought back with a ferocity that surprised even himself. He took a blow to the jaw, the taste of blood filling his mouth, but he didn't flinch then he saw an opening, a hockey stick lying discarded on the ground. He grabbed it, the smooth wood fitting perfectly in his grip.

As the men surged towards him, he swung the hockey stick, the impact a sickening thud and one by one they fell, their bodies dropping to the ground. Frank, breathing heavily, his grip firm around the hockey stick, continued his brutal assault until the alley was silent, the only sound his ragged breaths.

He looked around, his eyes scanning the darkness. No one had seen a thing and the alley was deserted, a stage set for a tragedy. The realization of what he had done washed over him in a wave of nausea and fear. He had killed them, all of them in a fit of uncontrollable rage, he had become a monster. He stumbled out of the alley, his mind reeling along with the image of the men's lifeless bodies seared into his memory. He didn't know what to do, where to go. He just knew he had to get away, to escape the horror of what he had done and that night, Frank didn't sleep. The images haunted him, the echo of the thuds ringing in his ears.

The rage that had consumed him in the alley was gone, replaced by a gnawing guilt, a chilling fear but something else had been born that night, something darker, something that would forever change the course of his life. The hockey stick, now stained with blood, was no longer just a sports implement. It was a weapon, a symbol of the violence that had been unleashed within him.

The adrenaline rush from the alley had subsided, replaced by a cold, calculating rage. Frank felt a twisted sense of purpose, a justification for his actions. He was ridding the world of its filth, one violent act at a time. His next target was close to home, someone who knew him, someone who trusted him. His old hockey coach.

He'd called his coach, suggesting a casual game with some old friends. The coach, a nice man who had once been a mentor, was thrilled at the idea of reconnecting and welcomed Frank into his home, the familiar scent of hockey equipment and old trophies filled the air. They reminisced about old games, laughed about past victories, the camaraderie masking the darkness that lurked within Frank and his game wasn't about hockey, it was a game of death, a twisted reenactment of the violence he had unleashed in the alley and as the coach turned to grab some beers from the fridge,

Frank seized his opportunity grabbing the hockey stick, the familiar weight comforting in his hands. The coach turned back, a look of confusion on his face, just as Frank swung the stick, the impact echoing through the house.

The coach dropped to the floor, his eyes wide with shock and disbelief and Frank didn't hesitate. He rained down blows with the hockey stick, the rage inside him finding its outlet in brutal, rhythmic swings. The room, once filled with laughter and friendly banter, was now a crime scene.

When it was over, Frank stood over his former mentor's lifeless body, his breath short, his heart pounding.

He felt no remorse, no regret. Only a chilling satisfaction. He had done it again. He had purged another stain from the world.

He left the house as quietly as he had entered, the hockey stick his silent accomplice. The game with his coach had been played, and Frank had won, in the most brutal and final way possible.

That was the day Frank began his killing spree, a vigilante turned murderer, the hockey stick his instrument of death and what started as a means of exerting control slowly morphed into a horrific cycle of violence and manipulation.

Frank soon found himself on a collision course with fate, and with every act of violence, he felt an adrenaline rush that momentarily filled the void left by his lost dreams.

He became known for his cunning and ability to evade capture, gaining notoriety as the "Phantom of St. Drake," and as the police closed in, Frank realized the depths to which he had sunk. The young athlete who once dreamed of glory on the ice had become a figure of terror, torn between the remnants of his past dreams and the reality of his present.

<u>The Hockey Stick</u>

<u>By ChoppTrigg</u>

The Murder Man Diaries

Murder Blades

Rudy's world revolved around skating. The feel of the wheels gliding across the floor, the wind whipping past as he carved turns, the sheer joy of movement – it was his lifeblood and being the owner of "Roll with Rudy," the city's most popular skate shop, cemented his place in the skating community. He was more than a businessman, he was an icon, a respected figure who lived and breathed the sport but beneath the surface of the charismatic entrepreneur lurked a volatile temper, a darkness that even Rudy himself barely understood and it was displayed one day when he had an altercation with Greg, the owner of the local roller rink, a rival and competitor in the cutthroat world of skating retail.

Their relationship was a constant push and pull, a mix of grudging respect and simmering animosity and today, that simmering tension had boiled over.

A shipment of high-end roller blades had gone missing, and Rudy was convinced Greg was behind it.

The argument had started in Greg's office, escalating quickly from accusations to insults.

Rudy's voice, usually jovial and friendly, was now laced with rage and Greg, equally furious, denied any involvement, their words echoing through the empty rink. The air was filled with anger as the two men locked in a battle of wills.

Then, something snapped causing Rudy lunged at Greg, the fight turning physical. They grappled, their bodies colliding with displays of skates and helmets and in the chaos, Rudy stumbled, his hand landing on a roller blade lying on a nearby shelf. He grabbed it, the smooth plastic and sharp wheels suddenly feeling like a weapon in his hand.

The fight continued, a blur of motion and fury then, in a moment of blinding rage, Rudy raised the roller blade high above his head slamming it down with full force, the impact a sickening thud. Greg flopped to the floor, his eyes wide with shock and pain.

Rudy stood over him, the roller blade still raised, his breath coming in ragged gasps. He looked down at Greg's lifeless body, the roller blade a trophy of his darkest moment.

The adrenaline that had fueled his rage quickly dissipated, replaced by a wave of horror.

He had killed Greg over a shipment of roller blades and the absurdity of it all was a crushing weight on his soul.

He had crossed a line, a point of no return. The thrill of the glide, the joy of skating, had been replaced by the chilling reality of his actions. He was no longer just Rudy, the skate shop owner. He was a killer.

Murder Blades

*T*he news of Greg's death burned the city like a wildfire. Disbelief rippled through the skating community, then spread outwards, engulfing the entire city.

Rudy, the friendly, charismatic owner of "Roll with Rudy," a man who had dedicated his life to the sport, a pillar of the skating world? It was unthinkable. Impossible. He was the last person anyone would suspect of such a violent act.

The police investigation was swift and thorough as they questioned everyone who knew Greg, everyone who had a connection to the roller rink. Rudy, naturally, was among those interviewed.

He cooperated fully, expressing his shock and sadness of Greg's death. He even offered his condolences to Greg's family, his grief appearing genuine.

When questioned about his whereabouts at the time of the murder, Rudy provided an alibi that seemed airtight. He had been at a local charity event, a well-publicized gathering attended by numerous prominent citizens. Several witnesses corroborated his story, placing him at the event throughout the evening. Security footage from the venue further confirmed his presence and the police investigated the alibi meticulously, but there was no way to poke holes in it. It was solid, unshakeable and despite the widespread suspicion and the whispers circulating about Rudy's volatile temper, the police found no concrete evidence linking him to the crime. No witnesses, no forensic clues, no connection whatsoever. Rudy's alibi, combined with the lack of any physical evidence, painted a picture of innocence, however unbelievable it seemed to those who knew him. The police were forced to consider other suspects, other motives.

The case of Greg's murder was quickly turning cold, a chilling reminder that sometimes, even when suspicion is strong, justice remains elusive and Rudy, the man with a secret hidden beneath his friendly facade, walked free.

Despite being cleared of suspicion, Rudy's mind was tormenting him. He felt an insatiable urge to skate, but every time he stepped onto the rink, he was haunted by the memories of that fateful night. Visions of Greg's blood on the slick floor played on a loop in his head, but in the hidden corners of Rudy's mind, a darker desire began to surface. What if he could silence anyone who might stand in his way, just like he had with Greg?

The thrill of getting away with Greg's murder fueled a dangerous transformation in Rudy.

The paranoia that had gnawed at him, the fear of exposure, morphed into something darker, a twisted sense of liberation. He had gotten away with it. He had silenced his rival and now he felt invincible.

The world was his for the taking, and anyone who stood in his way, anyone who posed a perceived threat, became a target.

Rudy's behavior grew increasingly erratic, his interactions with others shifting from friendly banter to thinly veiled threats. He became obsessed with control, determined to solidify his position at the top of the skating world.

Other skaters, especially those who dared to challenge his skills or his authority, felt the sting of his increasingly aggressive nature. He'd subtly undermine their performances, spread rumors about their character, anything to maintain his dominance and the owner of another skate shop, Darren, became a particular focus of Rudy's paranoia.

 Darren was a rising star in the community, his innovative designs and savvy marketing attracting a growing clientele and Rudy saw him as a direct competitor, a threat to his empire.

He decided to confront Darren, masking his true intentions with a pretense of reconciliation.

They met one evening, ostensibly to mend fences, to bridge the gap between their rival businesses.

The conversation started amicably enough, but the underlying tension was off the scale and as they discussed the market, their respective businesses, the talk inevitably turned to competition.

Rudy, his paranoia simmering just below the surface, felt a surge of anger.

He accused Darren of trying to steal his customers, of undermining his reputation.

Darren, surprised by the sudden shift in tone, tried to defend himself, but Rudy wasn't listening.

He saw red, the same blinding rage that had consumed him with Greg. The glint of a roller blade, lying within reach, caught his eye. The past repeated itself, a horrifying echo of violence and in a flash, Rudy grabbed the roller blade, the familiar weight and sharp edges triggering a primal instinct.

He lashed out, the roller blade connecting with Darren's face, the impact brutal and decisive.

Darren stumbled to the ground, his dreams and ambitions extinguished in a moment of senseless violence. Rudy in his rage, stood over his latest victim, the roller blade a chilling testament to his descent into madness. He had silenced another rival and he knew, with a chilling certainty, that this was just the beginning.

Murder Blades

*T*he police investigation into Darren's death mirrored the earlier investigation into Greg's. Detectives interviewed Rudy's friends, his acquaintances, anyone who had interacted with him in the days leading up to the murder. They questioned his alibi, scrutinized his demeanor, searched for any flicker of guilt, any slip-up that would connect him to the crime but Rudy remained calm, collected, his answers carefully rehearsed, his facade of innocence impenetrable. He knew the drill now. He had learned from his previous "success."

He played the grieving friend, the shocked member of the skating community, expressing his disbelief and sorrow at Darren's tragic demise, he even offered his assistance to the police, suggesting leads, pointing fingers at other potential suspects. He was a master of deception, a wolf in sheep's clothing, expertly manipulating the narrative, weaving a web of lies that obscured his dark deeds and as the days turned into weeks, and the police investigation stalled, the city became increasingly divided. The charismatic Rudy, the beloved figure in the skating world, couldn't possibly be a killer, some argued. He was a misunderstood artist, a passionate entrepreneur who had simply been in the wrong place at the wrong time, twice.

His supporters rallied behind him, defending his innocence, citing his contributions to the community, his friendly demeanor but some weren't so easily convinced.

People had began to talk behind closed doors. They spoke of Rudy's volatile temper, his intense rivalry with Darren, the strange coincidence of two skate shop owners meeting violent ends. They called him "Murder Blade's," a dark figure creeping after hours, a predator disguised as a pillar of the community.

The city was on edge, gripped by fear and suspicion. The once-unquestioned hero was now a figure of controversy, a symbol of the darkness that could hide behind a charming smile and Rudy, watching from the afar, felt a thrill of power, a perverse satisfaction at the chaos he had sown. He was playing a dangerous game and he was winning for now.

Murder Blades

*R*udy basked in his perceived invincibility.

He had outsmarted the police, manipulated the publics opinion, and silenced his rivals. He was untouchable, a phantom gliding through the city, leaving a trail of fear and suspicion in his wake and just as he began to believe in his own myth, a figure emerged, a force that threatened to expose his carefully constructed facade.

The Murder Man Diaries

Detective Shakira Denise, a woman with a sharp mind and an even sharper intuition, wasn't buying it. The pieces of the puzzle didn't fit.

Two seemingly unrelated deaths, both connected to the skating community, both shrouded in a cloud of doubt.

Something was off and her instincts keen from years of experience, screamed that there was a connection, a link that everyone else had missed.

Shakira Denise had became obsessed with the cases, her pursuit fueled by a relentless determination to uncover the truth as she poured over surveillance footage, meticulously analyzing every frame, searching for a flicker of recognition, a connection between Rudy and the victims. She delved into phone records, tracing calls, analyzing patterns, looking for any communication that would link Rudy to the crime scenes. She interviewed witnesses, re-interviewed those who had spoken to the police before, searching for inconsistencies, for details that had been overlooked.

Her colleagues dismissed her suspicions, chalking it up to a hunch, a gut feeling that lacked concrete evidence but Shakira Denise wouldn't be thrown off the trail.

She knew the truth was out there and she felt it in her bones, a certainty that grew stronger with each passing day.

Rudy wasn't just a suspect; he was the key and she was determined to unlock the secrets he so desperately tried to conceal. The truth was coming. It was only a matter of time.

Murder Blades

*T*he pieces of Shakira Denise investigation began to click into place forming a picture far more complex than she had initially imagined. Greg and Darren, the victims weren't just rival businessmen; they were partners in a clandestine operation, a black market for modified roller blades where they used their legitimate businesses as fronts, smuggling and selling illegal, dangerous equipment to the highest bidders.

The skating community, the community Rudy so fiercely protected, was being poisoned from within.

The realization hit Shakira Denise like a ton of bricks. Rudy wasn't a killer; he was a pawn, a man caught in the crossfire of a dangerous game. He had stumbled upon their secret, perhaps inadvertently and in his rage fueled by a desire to protect what he loved, he had become the instrument of their downfall. He wasn't a cold-blooded murderer he was a victim manipulated and transformed into the very monster he was fighting against and as Shakira Denise dug deeper, she uncovered a trail of evidence that exonerated Rudy and exposed Greg and Darren's illegal activities. Surveillance footage from their warehouses revealed the modified roller blades, their serial numbers matching those of blades linked to several accidents and injuries. Financial records showed a network of offshore accounts tracing the flow of money from their black-market sales.

Witness testimonies were previously dismissed as hearsay, now corroborated the evidence, painting a picture of two men driven by greed and a ruthless disregard for the safety of the skating community and the climax arrived with a dramatic confrontation. Shakira Denise, armed with irrefutable proof cornered the true culprits and associates of Greg and Darren who were still operating the black market. A tense standoff ensued, but Shakira Denise with the support of her fellow officers managed to apprehend them, bringing their illegal operation crashing down.

Simultaneously, Rudy, in a moment of chilling self-awareness, confronted the buried truth. He wasn't a hero, he was a product of the very darkness he had tried to extinguish.

He had become the monster they had created, a vigilante consumed by his own rage. The weight of his actions, the lives he had taken, crashed down on him, a crushing burden of guilt and regret.

Shakira Denise arrived at the scene, witnessed Rudy's internal struggle and his moment of reckoning. She saw not a killer, but a broken man, a victim of circumstance.

She stepped in, revealing the evidence she had uncovered, the truth that exonerated him and exposed the real criminals.

Rudy, his world shattered, his illusions destroyed, was finally free. He was no longer a killer, but a man who had been pushed to the brink, a man who had fought for what he believed in, even if his methods were tragically flawed and justice was served, not in the way anyone had expected, but in a way that revealed the complex shades of gray that existed even in the darkest corners of the city.

Murder Blades

The dust settled, the sound of violence blended with the background noise of the city. Rudy, stripped bare of his illusions, his rage finally extinguished, was left with the wreckage of his actions.

The truth, once a blinding revelation now settled into a chilling understanding. The real enemy hadn't been the rivals, the competitors, the perceived threats to his dominance.

The true danger had been creeping amongst the community he so fiercely loved, a darkness disguised as innovation, as ambition and progress.

Greg and Darren, the men he had killed, weren't just rivals they were corrupting the very heart of the skating world, poisoning it with their greed and the weight of his actions pressed down on Rudy, a burden heavier than any he had ever carried.

He had become a monster, a vigilante consumed by his own righteous fury and he was also a victim, a man manipulated and driven to violence by the very people he had sought to protect his community from. The realization was a bitter pill to swallow, a harsh lesson learned in the crucible of tragedy and as he began to rebuild his life, Rudy made a vow that he would re-establish his skate shop, not as a symbol of his power, not as a throne from which he could exert his will, but as a sanctuary for skaters. A place where the joy of skating could be celebrated without the shadow of fear, without the taint of corruption. He would use his experience, his hard-won wisdom, to guide young skaters, to teach them not just the skills of the sport, but also the importance of integrity and of humanity. He would be a reminder that the thrill of the glide and the exhilaration of the ride, should never come at the cost of one's life.

The day came when Rudy finally returned to the rink. The smooth surface, once a battleground, now beckoned him with a promise of peace. He laced up his skates, the familiar feel a comfort in the midst of his turmoil and as he stepped onto the rink, he felt a wave of emotion wash over him — grief, regret, but also a touch of hope. He wasn't just gliding on wheels he was embarking on a path toward redemption, a journey of healing and self-discovery.

He knew the road ahead would be long and difficult, but he was ready to face it, one graceful stride at a time. He would honor the memory of those he had wronged, not with violence, but with a commitment to building a better community, a community where the love of skating was a force for good, not a catalyst for destruction.

Murder Blades

By ChoppTrigg

The Murder Man Diaries

The Last Choice

*J*ustin Case, aide to the Secretary of State, moved through the polished halls of power with an air of quiet efficiency. His loyalty was unquestioned, his dedication absolute but behind the composed façade was a secret, a darkness inherited from his father, a legacy of blood that stretched back generations. The Case family curse assassination. Justin's father, known only as "7.62," was a legend in the game, a name spoke in fear and respect and now, that deadly mantle had fallen upon Justin as he navigated the treacherous currents of politics with the same precision and ruthlessness that defined his father's work. Each carefully worded memo, each strategic alliance, was a calculated move in a game where the stakes were life and death.

The killings, swift and clinical, were a necessary part of the job, a grim inheritance he couldn't escape and with every life extinguished, the weight of the curse grew heavier, pressing down on his soul, pushing him closer to the state of moral oblivion.

During a high-stakes mission, a delicate operation involving a foreign dignitary and a crucial treaty, Justin's carefully constructed world began to unravel. He eliminated the target with his usual efficiency leaving no trace or so he thought and in the the heat of the moment, a single, excruciating piece of evidence was left behind. His custom-made cufflink engraved with the Case family crest.

It was a careless mistake, a rookie error and it threatened to expose his double life

The Murder Man Diaries

shattering the carefully crafted illusion of Justin Case, the loyal aide.

The comfortable shadows he inhabited were suddenly filled with a harsh, unforgiving light as he was no longer just an assassin, he was a suspect, a loose end that needed to be tied and the FBI were closing in.

The discovery of the cufflink sent chills through the corridors of power. The authorities, the very people Justin served, were now on his trail and the gossip started, among few at first, then growing louder, more insistent and the name "7.62" resurfaced, linked to a series of unsolved murders, a ghost from the past suddenly made flesh and now, that ghost wore the face of Justin Case.

The Last Choice

The hunt began, swift and relentless. The scent of blood and the promise of a hefty reward is what drew the attention of bounty hunters from across the globe.

They swarmed the city, a pack of predators tracking their prey, the look on there faces after years of chasing criminals, scanned every alleyway and every darkened doorway. They were professionals, each with their own unique methods, but united by a single goal, to capture Justin Case.

They knew he was dangerous with a killer's instinct, one of their own turned rogue and they wouldn't hesitate to bring him down knowing what he was capable of and they soon found out.

The first encounter was a brutal round up of death. Six bounty hunters, confident in their numbers cornered Justin. They moved in unison, their weapons raised, their voices echoing and Justin was ready. He was a predator in his element, a master of the shadows as he moved with a speed that defied the eye, a blur of motion and violence and in the blink of an eye, the tables turned. In a flash a silenced pistol went off, a knife flashed and bodies fell to the concrete floor.

Six men all skilled hunters became the hunted, their lives snuffed in a matter of seconds and Justin vanished as quickly as he had appeared leaving behind a scene of carnage, a chilling testament to his deadly skills and the message was clear. Justin Case was not to be fucked with. He was not just a hunted animal, he was a cornered predator who would fight to the death.

The pressure mounted on Justin and the walls felt as if they were closing in around him. He was no longer just an assassin he was a fugitive running for his life. The roles had reversed and he found himself in a desperate fight for survival as he moved through the city like a wraith using his skills along with the training his father had instilled in him and how to evade his pursuers. He was a ghost among ghosts, a dark figure among figures, always two steps ahead but never truly safe and Justin wasn't just running, he was also on the hunt.

He knew the bounty hunters wouldn't stop until they had him and he wouldn't allow himself to be cornered.

He reversed the game using his skills to track them anticipating their moves and to eliminate them one by one therefore he became both the hunted and the hunter, a deadly paradox and every kill was a desperate attempt to stay alive, to protect the secret that threatened to shatter his carefully constructed world, the line between his inherited legacy and his current reality blurred, each kill pushing him further into the abyss making him more like his father, the infamous "7.62." and in doing so, had embraced the side he had tried so hard to escape.

Time was a relentless enemy, each tick of the clock a step closer to capture or death. Justin, knowing he couldn't face the storm alone, sought out Strawberry Jenkins, an old friend and forensic investigator who had once helped him erase his tracks. She was his only hope, a confidante who understood his secret and together, they pieced together a plan to clear his name, to expose the conspiracy that had turned him into a fugitive and just as they began to see a glimpse of light, tragedy struck, a chilling ambush orchestrated with ruthless precision by the relentless bounty hunters.

In the midst of the hunt Strawberry was caught in the crossfire and shot a number of times and as her blood stained the cold concrete she took her last breath and clutched Justin's hand, her eyes filled with a desperate plea.

She whispered, "Face your demons and understand the curse. It's not what you think."

Her words replayed in Justin's mind. He was alone again with the weight of his past and the loss of his friend crushing him. He stood at a crossroads trying to define his fate. He could turn himself in, face the consequences of his family's legacy and accept the punishment for his sins or he could fight and take down the bounty hunters who had taken Strawberry from him then delve into the depths of his family's dark past in search of the truth behind the curse that had haunted his lineage for generations.

Driven by vengeance and a desperate need to understand his own nature, Justin plunged into the abyss of his family history. He traced his lineage back through dusty records and forgotten stories and as he dug deeper, a shocking truth began to emerge.

The Murder Man Diaries

A twist in the curse that changed everything he thought he knew. The Case family legacy wasn't just about assassination, it was about survival.

His ancestors hadn't been simply killers they had been protectors and guardians of a secret, a truth that powerful forces wanted to keep buried and now Justin found himself caught in the middle of a centuries-old conspiracy, a battle between light and darkness where the lines between good and evil were thin and his own destiny hung in the balance.

The final confrontation was on pins and needles with the air thick with anticipation. Justin, driven by the revelations unearthed in his family's hidden chamber, stood poised to confront not just the bounty hunters, but the architects of his family's "curse."

The journals, filled with his ancestors' very words had shattered his understanding of his legacy. He wasn't a product of violence; he was a pawn in a game far older, far more sinister. The "Curse" wasn't a bloodline of assassins it was a carefully crafted narrative, a lie perpetuated by a powerful organization to maintain its grip on control. The murders weren't acts of inherited malice they were orchestrated eliminations, threats to the organization's power disguised as the work of a family curse.

The leader of the bounty hunters stepped forward, his face a mask of cold calculation. He was a high-ranking government official, a man Justin had trusted, a man who had manipulated him from the behind the desk but the true shock came with the revelation of another player in this deadly game and that was Strawberry Jenkins. She wasn't an ally, she was a puppet master pulling the strings from behind the scenes. She had posed as a friend offering support while secretly ensuring the "Curse" remained active, a convenient cover for the organization's dirty work.

Her betrayal cut deep, a wound that went beyond the physical battles he had fought but Justin was no longer the naive pawn they had manipulated. He had seen the truth, understood the game and now he was ready to play it on his own terms. He turned the tables on his pursuers exposing the organization's secrets, revealing their manipulation of his family and their use of murder to maintain power. The climactic showdown wasn't just a physical battle it was a war for truth, a fight to reclaim his family's name and break the cycle of violence that had defined their legacy for generations and in the end, Justin didn't succumb to the darkness he rose above it.

He embraced his pasta and his skills but he redefined their purpose. He used his training along with his knowledge he'd obtained, not to kill but to protect, to expose and dismantle the corrupt system that had sought to exploit him and his family.

He redeemed his family's name, not through violence, but through justice and in the end the curse was broken, not by denying his lineage but by understanding it and turning its dark legacy into a force for good. Justin Case, the descendant of assassins, became Justin Case, the breaker of curses, the champion of truth.

The Last Choice

By ChoppTrigg

The Murder Man Diaries

Made in the USA
Columbia, SC
24 March 2025